"While Coupland still has a youthful flair to his prose, *The Gum Thief* reveals a more layered and interesting side of the writer that we've rarely seen before." —*Edmonton Journal*

"Douglas Coupland is the thinking man's Jerry Seinfeld. . . . Correction: Douglas Coupland is the feeling man's Jerry Seinfeld." —*National Post*

"Coupland shines, the story is humorous, frenetic, focused and curiously affecting." —*Publishers Weekly* (starred review)

"An innovative, fast-paced story told without the bells and whistles of *JPod,* but just as topical and lively and relevant." —*The Globe and Mail*

"With *The Gum Thief,* author Douglas Coupland has pulled off a clever heist, appropriating Edward Albee's iconic play *Who's Afraid of Virginia Woolf?,* [and] using it as fodder for a satirical novel-within-a-novel." —*The Gazette* (Montreal)

"Sharp, witty and fast-paced." —*Winnipeg Free Press*

"Right from the get-go we're deep in Coupland country with *The Gum Thief.* . . . No one else quite captures the dystopian malaise of our post-postmodernist consumer-junkie culture quite like he does. Call it CoMo: Coupland Modernism." —*Quill & Quire* (starred review)

"Douglas Coupland is today a sharp, satirical writer and artist who has prolifically mined the vein of pop nihilism first exposed in his 1991 novel, *Generation X.* (His latest, *The Gum Thief,* makes clear that the vein has not been tapped out.)" —*The New York Times*

"*The Gum Thief* is both hilarious and clever." —*The Georgia Straight*

Douglas
Coupland
The Gum Thief

VINTAGE CANADA

VINTAGE CANADA EDITION, 2008

Published in Canada by Vintage Canada, a division of Random House
of Canada Limited, Toronto, in 2008. Originally published in hardcover
in Canada by Random House Canada, a division of Random House of
Canada Limited, Toronto, in 2007. Distributed by Random House
of Canada Limited, Toronto.

Vintage Canada and colophon are registered trademarks of Random House
of Canada Limited.

www.randomhouse.ca

Library and Archives Canada Cataloguing in Publication

Coupland, Douglas
    The gum thief / Douglas Coupland.

ISBN 978-0-307-35627-7

    I. Title.
PS8555.O8253G84 2008   C813'.54   C2007-906934-7

Printed and bound in Canada

10 9 8 7 6 5 4 3 2 1

Q: Brother, are you headed home?
A: Brother, aren't we always headed home?

—*Question used by Masons to identify themselves*
among strangers

Roger

A few years ago it dawned on me that everybody past a certain age—regardless of how they look on the outside—pretty much constantly dreams of being able to escape from their lives. They don't want to be who they are any more. They want *out*. This list includes Thurston Howell the Third, Ann-Margret, the cast members of *Rent*, Václav Havel, space shuttle astronauts and Snuffleupagus. It's universal.

Do *you* want out? Do you often wish you could be somebody, *any*body, other than who you are—the you who holds a job and feeds a family—the you who keeps a relatively okay place to live and who still tries to keep your friendships alive? In other words, the you who's going to remain pretty much the same until the casket?

There's nothing wrong with me being me, or with you being you. And in the end, life's pretty tolerable, isn't it? *Oh, I'll get by.* We all say that. *Don't worry about me.* Maybe I'll get drunk and go shopping on eBay at eleven at night, and maybe I'll buy all kinds of crazy crap I won't remember I bid on the next morning, like a ten-pound bag of mixed coins from around the world or a bootleg tape of Joni Mitchell performing at the Calgary Saddledome in 1981.

I used the phrase "a certain age." What I mean by this is the age people are in their heads. It's usually thirty to thirty-four. Nobody is forty in their head. When it comes to your internal age, chin wattles and relentless liver spots mean nothing.

In my mind, I'm always thirty-two. In my mind, I'm drinking sangria beachside in Waikiki; Kristal from Bakersfield is flirting with me, while Joan, who has yet to have our two kids, is up in our hotel room fetching a pair of sunglasses that don't dig into her ears as much. By dinnertime, I'm going to have a mild sunburn, and when I return home from that holiday, I'll have a $5K salary bonus and an upgraded computer system waiting for me at my office. And if I dropped fifteen pounds and changed gears from sunburn to suntan, I could look halfway okay. Not even okay: *hot*.

Do I sound regretful?

Okay, maybe a bit.

Okay, let's face it—I'm king of the exit interview. And Joan was a saint. My curse is that I'd rather be in pain than be wrong.

I'm sad at having flubbed the few chances I had to make bold strokes in life. I'm learning to cope with the fact that it was both my laziness and my useless personal moral code that cheated me out of seizing new opportunities. Listen to me: *flubbed chances and missed opportunities*: I gloss past them both in almost the same breath. But there was no gloss when it was all coming down. It's taken me what—five years?—to simply get used to the idea that I've blown things. I'm grieving, grieving hard-core. The best part of my life is gone, and what remains is whizzing past so quickly I feel like I'm Krazy-Glue'ed onto a mechanical bull of a time machine.

I can't even escape in my dreams. My dreams used to be insulated by pink fibreglass, but maybe two jobs ago my sense of failure ripped a hole through the insulation and began wrecking them. I dreamed it was that Monday afternoon in the 1990s when my high school buddy turned vampire stockbroker, Lars, phoned me a week after my mother's funeral—a week!—and told me to put everything and anything I might have inherited into Microsoft stock. I told him our friendship was over. I told him he was a parasite. And if Microsoft had sunk into the earth's crust and vanished, I might have actually forgiven Lars, but that didn't happen. Their sack-of-shit operating system conquered the planet, and my $100,000 inheritance from my mother, put into Microsoft, would currently be worth a smidge over $13 million.

I get the Microsoft dream about once a week now.

But okay, there's some good stuff in my life. I love my spaniel, Wayne, and he loves me. What a name for a dog, *Wayne*—like he's my accountant. The thing is, dogs only hear vowels. It's a fact. When I call Wayne in for the night, he doesn't hear the W or the N. I could simply yell out *Ayyyyyyyyyyy* and he'd still show up. For that matter, I suppose I could also simply yell out *Paaaaiiiiiiiiiiin* and he'd show up. At my last job, I told Mindy the comptroller how much I loved Wayne, and you know what she said to me? She said, "Dogs are like people, except you can legally kill dogs if they bug you." Which makes you wonder—one household in three has a dog in it, but all they are (from the Mindy perspective) is semi-disposable family members. We need to have laws to make killing dogs illegal. *But what about cats?* Okay, cats, too. *What about snakes? Or sea monkeys?*

I draw the line at sea monkeys. I draw lines everywhere. It's what makes people think I'm Mister Difficult. For example, people in the ATM machine lineup who stand too far away from the dispenser forfeit their right to be next in line. You know the people I mean—the ones who stay fifty feet away so they don't look like they're trying to see your PIN number. Come *on.* I look at these people, and I think, *Man, you must feel truly guilty about something to make you broadcast your sense of guilt to the world with your freakish lineup philosophy.* And so I simply stand in front of them and go next. That teaches them.

What else? I also believe that if someone comes up behind you on the freeway and flashes their lights to get you to move into the slow lane, they deserve whatever punishment you dole out to them. I promptly slow down and drive at the same speed as the car beside me so that I can punish Speed Racer for his impertinence.

Actually, it's not the impertinence I'm punishing him for, it's that he let other people know what he wanted.

Speed Racer, my friend, never ever let people know what you want. Because if you do, you might as well send them engraved invitations saying, "Hi, this is what I want you to prevent me from ever having."

Bitter.

I am *not* bitter.

And even if I was, at least if you're bitter you know where you stand.

Okay, that last sentence came out wrong. Let me rephrase it:

At least if you're bitter, you know that you're like everybody else.

Strike that last effort, too. How about: At least if you're bitter, you know that you're a part of the family of man. You know that you're not so hot, but you also know that your experience is universal. "Universal" is such a great word. You know that we live in a world of bitter cranks—a world of aging bitter cranks who failed and who are always thirty-two in their own heads.

Failures.

But bitterness doesn't always mean failure. Most rich people I've met are bitter too. So, as I say, it's universal. Rejoice!

I was once young and fresh and dumb, and I was going to write a novel. It was going to be called *Glove Pond*. What a name—*Glove Pond*. I don't remember the inspiration, but the words have always sounded to me like the title of a novel or movie from England—like *Under Milk Wood*, by Dylan Thomas—or a play written by someone like Tennessee Williams. *Glove Pond* was to be populated with characters like Elizabeth Taylor and Richard Burton, movie stars from two generations ago, with killer drinking problems, teeter-tottering sexuality and soft, unsculpted bodies—from back before audiences figured out that muscle tone, not a press release, determines sexiness. *Glove Pond*'s main characters screamed and brawled and shrieked witty, catty, vicious things at each other. They drank like fish, screwed like minks and then caught each other in the act of screwing strangers like minks. At that point, they'd say even wittier things than before. They were wit machines. In the end, all the characters were crazy and humanity was doomed. The End.

I just googled "Glove Pond" and here's what I got:

> **www.amateurmicroscopy.net . . . Index to Articles**
> . . . Part 1: Introduction and Webcam Modifications. If ever a subject and a method of recording that subject fit together like a hand in a **glove, pond** "micro-critters" and videomicrography are an ideal fit.

Look at this: no one has ever put the two words together before—a comma in between "glove" and "pond" doesn't count as a true connection. So I still get dibs on *Glove Pond*!

Bethany

I'm the dead girl whose locker you spat on somewhere between recess and lunch.

I'm not really dead, but I dress like I want to be. There's something generic about girls like me: we hate the sun, we wear black, and we feel trapped inside our bodies like a nylon fur mascot at a football game. I wish I were dead most of the time. I can't believe the meat I got stuck with, and where I got stuck and with whom. I wish I were a ghost.

And FYI, I'm not in school any more, but the spitting thing was real: a little moment that sums up life. I work in a Staples. I'm in charge of restocking aisles 2-North and 2-South: Sheet Protectors, Indexes & Dividers, Notebooks, Post-It Products, Paper Pads, Specialty Papers and "Social Stationery." Do I hate this job? Are you nuts? Of course I hate it. How could you not hate it? Everyone who works with me is either already damaged or else they're embryos waiting to be damaged, fresh out of school and slow as a 1999 modem. Just because you've been born and made it through high school doesn't mean society can't still abort you. Wake up.

Let me try to say something positive here. For balance. Staples allows me to wear black lipstick to work.

I was waiting for the bus this morning, and there was a sparrow sitting in the azalea beside the bus shelter. I looked at it and it yawned . . . this tiny little wisp of heated sparrow yawn breath rose up from the branch. And the thing is, I began yawning too—so yawning is contagious not only from person to person, but from species to species. How far back was it that our primordial ancestors forked into two directions, one that became mammals and one that became birds? Five hundred million years ago? So we've been yawning on earth for half a billion years.

Speaking of biology, I think cloning is great. I don't understand why churchy people get so upset about it. God made the originals, and cloning is only making photocopies. Big woo. And how can people get upset about evolution? Someone had to start the ball rolling; it's only natural to try to figure out the mechanics of *how* it got rolling. Relax! One theory doesn't exclude the other.

Yesterday this guy from work, Roger, said it was weird that we human beings, who've evolved way more than anything else on earth, still have to share the place with all the creatures that remain unevolved, like bacteria and lizards and bugs. Roger said human beings should have a special roped-off VIP section for people only. I got so mad at him for being such an ignorant shit. I told him that roped-off VIP areas do, in fact, exist, and they're called parking lots—if Roger wanted to be such an environmental pig about things, he should go stand in the parking lot for a few days and see how much fun *that* is.

Calm down, Bethany. Look out the window.

I'm looking out the window.

I'm going to focus on nature. Looking at plants and birds cools my brain.

It's late afternoon right now, and the crows, a hundred thousand of them from everywhere in the city, are all flying to roost for the night in their mega-roost, an alder forest out on the highway in Burnaby. They go there every night, and I don't know why. They're party animals, I suppose. Crows are smart. Ravens are smarter. Have you ever seen a raven? They're like people, they're so smart. I was fourteen and collecting seashells up the coast one afternoon, and a pair of ravens landed on a log beside me and followed me around the beach, hopping from log to log. They were talking to each other—I mean chatter-chatter talking—and they were obviously discussing *me*. Ever since then, I've firmly believed that intelligent life exists everywhere in the universe; in fact, the universe is designed specifically to foster life wherever and whenever possible.

I also think that if ravens lived to seventy-two instead of seven, they'd have conquered the planet millions of years ago. They're that smart. Raven intelligence evolved differently than human intelligence, but it still reached a human place. Aliens may well think and behave like ravens or crows.

And a final thing about crows—I had no idea I'd be going on like this—is that they look black to us, but to birds, they're as insanely coloured as parakeets and peacocks—human colour perception is missing a small patch of the spectrum that only birds can see. Imagine if we could see the world like birds, even briefly. Everything would be wondrous. Which is another reason why I only wear black. Who knows what you're missing when you look at me.

It's five minutes later.

My mother called and asked if I would consider going with her to visit the Hubble Telescope in California. I thought the Hubble was in outer space, but it turns out it has a twin, in Yreka, in northern California.

My mother said people who didn't believe in anything had visited the telescope and it had made them proud to be alive. She said that, instead of the stars being these mean, cold, bleak little jabs of white light, the universe was like a vast, well-maintained aquarium. The stars weren't points of light, but angel fish and jellyfish and sea horses and anemones. And I thought about it, and damn the woman, she's right.

I told her that people always treat me like an alien; I've always expected to be treated as such, and it's not a very glamorous sensation.

This, naturally, sparked a fight with Mom. *Why can't I try to fit in?*

If I'm still wearing black lipstick at twenty-four, she ought to have abandoned hope of my ever normalizing.

After we hung up, I thought, what if she'd died right there on the spot, right at the end of that phone call. The last thing she ever would have said to me would have been, *Imagine, Bethany, the universe is indeed a beautiful place. If you doubt me, go check for yourself.*

Roger

Sorrow!

Sorrow is everywhere—a bruise that never yellows and never fades, a weed that chokes the crop. Sorrow is every old person who ever died alone in a small, shitty room. Sorrow is alive in the streets and in the shopping malls. Sorrow in space stations and theme parks. In cyberspace; in the Rocky Mountains; in the Mariana Trench. All this *sorrow.*

And here I am in the cemetery eating my lunch: baloney on Wonder Bread, too much yellow mustard, no lettuce or tomato, an apple and a beer. I believe that the dead speak to us, but I don't think they do it with words. They use the materials they have at hand—a gust of air, a gold ripple on an otherwise still lake, or inside a dozing stem some sap is tickled and a flower blooms that would never have opened otherwise.

The sky rains and the world shines, tombstones like rhinestones, the grass like glass. There is a breeze.

Joan tried to be so matter-of-fact about it all when she got the news: cancer of the spleen. What the hell is a spleen?

A spleen is a cartoon body part, not something a real person has, let alone something that gets sick and kills.

Joan tried to tell me that everybody who's ever lived has had cancer lots of times—even a fetus gets cancer—except our bodies almost always get rid of it before it spreads. Cancer is what we call those bits our bodies fail to slough off. I found some comfort in that. It made cancer feel everyday and approachable. *Universal*. I wanted to reach inside Joan and pluck out the cancer—and maybe while I was there I'd remove gold coins and keys and tropical birds—and I'd show you the surprises all of us conceal within.

I think emotions affect your body as much as X-rays and vitamins and car crashes. And whatever it is I'm feeling right now, well, God only knows what parts of my body are being demolished. And I deserve it. Because I'm not a good person—because I'm a bad person who also happens to be lost.

Oh! To travel back ten years—to when I still thought of myself as a good person and before I realized I was lost. Every moment felt like I was getting away with something. Every moment felt like five o'clock quitting time. Paradise!

You know how I met Joan? I was coming back from lunch with Alex and Marty. I'd had three glasses of red, and I knew it wouldn't be too smart to show up at the office—it was the tail end of the days when you could still plausibly drink during lunch and not immediately be suspended, and I didn't want to push it—this was my third job in five years. So I pretended I had to pick something up from the dry cleaners. It was a sweater-optional weather day, and the sun came out from behind a cloud and I was standing on the corner of Seymour and Nelson in a wonderful liquid yellowness. I felt like I was being teleported into the sun, and the heat on my skin felt like music. Then the sun went behind the clouds, and I felt like I was locked inside an airliner's bathroom. And then I closed my eyes and opened them again and across the street was a fortune teller.

What the hey!

So I walked over, laid down a five and said, "Fill me in."

The fortune teller certainly wasn't cultivating an aura of mystery. She dressed like her welfare cheque had just arrived and she was off to buy a carton of smokes for her six illegitimate toddlers: sweats; no makeup; a pair of men's brown leather shoes.

But I still wanted my fortune told. It's a mood you get maybe once a decade, like a thirst, and once you have it, you have to slake it. So I pressed forward. "What can you tell me?"

She looked at me like I was homework. She grabbed my hand, pressed the meat of my thumb for a few seconds, looked up at me and said, "I see you sitting in a glade, all of the creatures of the forest sitting around you. There's a blue jay on your left palm, a black squirrel on your right—it's dozing—it's resting, it feels completely at peace."

That's not what I was expecting, but I liked the way the words made the inside of my head feel.

She looked down at my palm, then back up at me and went on: "You were trouble as a teenager, and you probably pushed your parents too far, and they probably gave you up for lost."

She was good.

She said, "You were about twenty, and you saw something that scared you into changing your ways. What was it?"

"Aren't you supposed to be telling me?"

"A car accident."

Shit, she *was* good.

"How many people were killed?" she asked.

"Four."

"Four people—and afterwards you went to your parents' house. You said to them something along the lines of, *Mom, Dad, I've seen the error of my ways, and I've decided I no longer want to be the person I was before. I'm going to be someone new now, someone better, somebody I can respect.* Your mother cried."

Traffic and people thrummed around us, but they might as well have been on a TV muted in the background. I didn't know what to say.

"The thing is," she continued, "you changed only a little bit, and only for a little while. You lacked the courage to follow through on the criminal promise of your teens, and you were too lazy to become a genuinely good person. You wonder why I look at you funny, well, now you know why."

I was tipsy, so I said, "I know about my past. Tell me about my future."

She said, "What am I supposed to tell you—that your future's going to be different, or better? I can't, because you're never going to change. You may have a red-haired son and a left-handed daughter. You may be stung by a jellyfish in Mexico and die within an hour. But so what? In your head, you're this neither-here-nor-there person. The experiences won't change you. Who cares?"

She said, "You think I'm trailer trash, but so? What of it? I have a certain power, but having it doesn't mean I have to embrace it. Most of the time I reject my powers, but today I needed money, and that money is going to come from you. A hundred dollars. Pay me now."

"Why should I?"

"Because otherwise I'll tell you even more things about yourself you'd rather not know. Buy my silence."

I did.

She folded up my five twenties and her card table and walked away.

Then, from behind me, a woman's voice said, "I bet you like animals."

I turned around and there was Joan, with a Jack Russell on a leash straining to sniff curbside newspaper boxes.

"Huh?"

"Animals. I bet you talk to animals all the time, whenever you see them. Like right here, right now."

She was the same age as me, but without the mileage. She looked like Jane, from the Dick and Jane books, grown up, apple-cheeked, healthy and itching to correct my grammar. She saw that I was maybe a disaster, and yet she approached me. *She* began our dance together. I looked at her dog, Astro. "Hey there, boy. Yeah, I do love animals." I scratched him behind his ears. "Why would your mistress be telling me that?"

"Why?" she asked. "Because people who talk to animals are people who are easily disinhibited. Certain situations take them out of themselves—talking to animals, or talking to fortune tellers. A fortune teller gives you permission to relax and not keep everything plugged up. You can tell them anything. And once it's over, back in goes the plug and you feel better for having vented."

"You heard her?"

"I couldn't help it. Young Astro here had to do his business and I had to wait."

"She saw you there, listening, the whole time?"

"Yup."

"And you still want to talk to me?"

Brendan indeed had red hair, and Zoë is left-handed.

But I've never gone to Mexico, never will.

Bethany (for real)

Sparrows!

Sparrows are everywhere!

At McDonald's! On the park benches! On branches!

Roger, what a complete loser you are for leaving your diary in the coffee room. As if people weren't going to find it, let alone *me*. I'm totally creeped out by your description of me and my mother and my life. Creeped out to the point where I could get you fired. But that would mean acknowledging you in a way that would fit too neatly into your self-described loser profile. I can hear it now: *That caustic little slut got me fired because I wrote about her black lipstick.* You talked about my *body*, Roger—and what I felt like being inside my body. What kind of perv are you?

But the bit about the sparrow was nice, I have to admit. And I've actually seen birds yawn before, but then I think of you staring at me at a bus stop staring at sparrows and I get creeped out. BTW, you saw me at a bus stop and drove by when you could have driven me to work? Nice one.

And what's with you stealing all my comments about birds and biology? We have to talk about *something* in the staff room—besides Darrell and Raheed and Shawn bitching about customers, especially the needy ones in Hand-Helds & PDAs. Customers are all the same. They're all little children. I hate children. Children are like small brain-damaged adults with no attention spans and no capacity for conversation. Children should be sent away to school until they turn twenty-one and can speak normally. Darrell, Raheed and Shawn should also be sent away until they learn to speak properly, but that'd be age eighty-four, if ever. Man, their bitching drives me nuts. And how dare Shawn tell you about the spit on my locker in grade twelve!

And don't think I didn't notice that last Thursday you got yourself transferred from Laser Printers into stocking the bond paper so you could drink while you work. I was in the staff room, and I gagged on a saltine cracker and reached for your water bottle, which was on the counter, and got a mouthful of vodka. Yes, you're in winner territory, Roger. And I heard you sold some geek $5K worth of computer crap and forgot to tell him it wouldn't work on Macs. Chris had to stay late and process the returns, and he cursed your existence for an hour.

I'm sorry people in your life seem to have died or left you or something. So I won't be a total witch here. And two kids—really? Because, Roger, you can barely knot a tie onto one of your semi-washed shirts every morning, so I have to wonder if your kids get fed properly.

That was mean. Sorry. Shawn says you live alone.

My mother—you make her sound like a mystic who goes through life singing songs and making people feel campfire good about themselves. Please! She's tortured me my entire life, and she's also the inhabitant of a faraway land called Uselessness. Last week she pushed the wrong buttons and microwaved a bun for ten hours, and the condo smelled like an electrical fire for days.

Yes, I know what you're thinking: *Bethany lives with her mother.* Why is it okay for guys to stay home forever, but if a girl does she's damaged goods? Have you priced condos lately? And working at Staples is a career? I can't believe the government even classifies what we do as a job. A job is something you can do for life. A job has some dimension of hope to it. Setting up fresh little sheets of white paper for people to use to test magic markers is not a hope scenario. All people ever draw is squiggles. It'd be fun if they wrote the occasional *fuck* or drew anarchy symbols. I still can't believe people ever *pay* for pens. Talk about the world's most shopliftable item. Staples must die.

At least your waste-case diary is something I can fume about while I'm installing the Halloween display this afternoon. (Note: What kind of person buys a jar of orange and black jellybeans to "celebrate" Halloween? Everyone thinks that because I wear black lipstick I live for Halloween or something. It's such an embarrassing holiday. They should call it Alter Ego Day—everyone dresses up as who they'd rather be instead of themselves. Sort of like what you said about people wanting out—or people wanting to be anything except what and who they are. I'd dress up as an ivory-billed woodpecker. Imagine everybody wondering if you existed, hoping you did, longing for a quick glance of you.)

BTW, did you see the tattoo of the devil on Shawn's ankle? I used to think that tattoo = slut, but now I think it's the total opposite. When you get a tattoo, it means you want your sexual partner to remember you and bond with you—which is to say, it's more about monogamy than it is about sluttitude. Nature is crafty, but you know, black lipstick or not, I draw the line at tattoos. Because I like my skin to be deathly white. Michael Jackson white. I want it to look like it's easy to bruise. I want it to look like I taste like almond paste.

I can't believe I'm writing this to a total perv like you. Well, it's something to kill time here at Shtooples.

Here's what I'm going to do. When we see each other, neither of us is allowed to acknowledge that we've written or read these things we've written and read. We have to pretend we're cats and dogs, like normal. It'll make life interesting, which is a supreme challenge in this place. Boy, would I like to open a stockroom door one day and find people doing something shocking.

Describe something shocking, Bethany . . .

Okay, how about Chris using an oversize oak peppermill to grind crack cocaine onto Shawn's rectum because Shawn's nose is so coked out that she's had to find a new absorbent membrane. That's shocking. That'd be fun to see. Or maybe Kyle using words longer than three syllables. But guys like Kyle don't need words to succeed in life, merely a pair of tight jeans and a dab of hair product.

What's on today's To-Do list? Besides the Halloween display, I have to redo Jamie's lame "Make Your Office

Your Home" display down by the business furniture section. All she had to do was put coffee cups on a desktop and set a wacky stuffed animal beside the PC monitor. Instead, she created a scarecrow-ish stuffed body with a head made of pantyhose filled with bubble wrap, the face drawn with a bingo-daubing marker. It's . . . disturbing.

BTW, you owe me, buster. I was walking down your aisle, and I had to reorganize a pile of Sharpie pens into their correct nooks because somebody had scrambled them this morning—some brave anarchist in training. I also saved you from a future shit storm by cleaning off the dust and fingerprints that were all over the cardboard box display for Zebra mechanical pencils.

Remember, no acknowledging to my face that you've read this.

Glove Pond begins

"You're drunk again."

"I'm always drunk, you combative harridan. Shush."

"Don't shush me, you failure of a man. You manfail-ure."

"At least I don't sleep with a lawn sprinkler repair-man as an act of retaliation sex."

"At least he's a man."

"Meaning what, Gloria?"

"You figure it out. I'm having more Scotch."

Gloria and Steve were being drunk and witty. Daylight savings had just ended, and the world was get-ting dark way too soon. They had each emerged from their respective realms to forage for liquor in the living room. It was a space defined by its rice-paper-thin Persian rugs and homely, expensive oak furniture made in the late nineteenth century by underfed, uneducated children with scurvy in rural Michigan factories. Random felts of house dust rested where Gloria had not deigned to drag a chamois during her random bouts of chatelaine energy.

The year was 2007. Steve's head felt like crumpled paper after six hours of departmental meetings. Gloria's blood chemicals were shooting in all directions after an unexpectedly cancelled tryst with Leonard, the director of the local dinner theatre. She would be appearing in three weeks as the lead in the local dinner theatre production of *Lady Windermere's Fan*, and she was insecure about her adequacy for the role.

Steve barked, "More Scotch. I don't feel drunk enough." He filled his glass and added one ice cube as an afterthought.

"Are you sure you want an ice cube in there? It might dilute your buzz."

"Why is it that all we do is battle?" He sighed, rattled his ice cube and coughed.

Back in her thirties, one by one, all of Gloria's other powerful emotions had gone out to get a pack of cigarettes and had never returned. Only anger remained. "We don't battle. We drink. It's different with us."

Steve looked at his watch. "The guests will be here in a half-hour. What are we having?"

"I don't know. I'll figure something out."

"We have guests coming over and you haven't figured it out yet?"

"No."

Roger

It's amazing how you can be a total shithead, and yet your soul still wants to hang out with you. Souls ought to have the legal right to bail once you cross certain behaviour thresholds: *I draw the line at cheating at golf; I draw the line at theft over $100,000; I draw the line at bestiality.* Imagine all the souls of the world, out on the sides of highways, all of them hitchhiking to try to find new places to live, all of them holding signs designed to lure you into selecting them as a passenger:

> . . . I sing!
> . . . I tell jokes.
> . . . I know shiatsu.
> . . . I know Katharine Hepburn.

I don't deserve a soul, yet I still have one. I know because it hurts.

However, earlier today at the Oasis Car Wash I bumped into an old friend from high school, Teddy, who had become a psychiatrist. While ex-cons buffed our rear-view mirrors and stole sunglasses and pocket change, I asked him if he'd reached any broad conclusions about humanity.

He asked me, "What kind of conclusions?"

"You know, that everybody on earth—not merely your patients—that everybody's a mess."

He perked up. "Oh, good God, man, get real. Everybody's a *disaster*."

His Chrysler 300 popped out of the buffing bay, and we said goodbye. I felt a thousand percent good for the first time in months. Having the same illness as everybody else truly is the definition of health.

Why, you may ask, do I spend the peanuts I make at work on a car wash? Because it makes me feel good. Because it was payday. Because my car is the one thing in my life that's working. It's a Hyundai Sonata, and nothing ever goes wrong with it. It's drop-dead boring but it *works*. I identify with it.

I just looked up and out the staff room door to see that Shawn is dressed as Wonder Woman. She's tit-proud, and she works it. I think if human beings had genuine courage, they'd wear their costumes every day of the year, not just on Halloween. Wouldn't life be more interesting that way? And now that I think about it, why the heck don't they? Who made the rule that everybody has to dress like sheep 364 days of the year? Think of all the people you'd meet if they were in costume every day. People would be so much easier to talk to—like talking to dogs. *Hey, cool costume! I dig vampires too. Let's go out for a beer.* Halloween costumes are another disinhibiting device, like fortune-telling and talking to dogs that belong to strangers.

Me? I'd dress like a matador. I can still cut a figure if I skip sugars and carbs for a month. Carrying a sword would be a kick. I'd always be wondering what it's like to stab a large animal, to see blood on the steel. I'd be . . . man, I reread the last two sentences. Psycho time.

Maybe all I want to do is carry a visible weapon.

There, that would be my costume. I'd be dressed the same way I am now, but I'd have a holster with a handgun. I'd be the Guy Who May or May Not Go Cuckoo for Cocoa Puffs at Any Moment.

Yet again, psycho time. I am not psycho. But I caught a glimpse of myself in the men's room mirror, and what I saw did disturb me: a puffy-looking forty-three—yellowing skin under the light of the lone fluorescent tube; dandruff; red patches on my scalp where I scratch my seborrhea. No wonder I've become invisible to people under thirty. Put my body inside the Hyundai and I'm the Invisible Man. I could commit any crime, and when cops interviewed witnesses and asked them who did it, all they'd remember is, "Some guy in a car."

Some guy dressed as Cupid just poked his head in the door and asked where we sell the jumbo cans of Maxwell House coffee. (Question: who buys coffee at an office supply store?)

And then Cupid left for Aisle 3-South, and I'm sitting here wondering.

Wondering what?

Wondering about Cupid and his arrows. Wondering if I still have the capacity to fall in love. Did I write that last sentence? What's next—growing breasts? And yet again I'm reminded of the pursed-lipped fortune teller I met on the street corner years ago. If you don't change, then what's the point of anything happening to you? It'll still be happening to an unchanged person.

Glove Pond, once again

"We can't serve guests canned soup for dinner. I'll be the laughingstock of the English department."

"You're not already? And besides, we don't have any canned soup."

"Jesus, Gloria, you're supposed to be witty. At all times. Hey, what's in here . . . ?" Steve fumbled through the tin foil drawer and found a bottle of gin. "Gin?"

"It's for when I'm too lazy to go to the liquor cabinet."

"Let's peel and boil some potatoes."

"We don't have any potatoes. We're broke. We spend all of our money on Scotch. We can't even order pizza."

"Let's get the guests so drunk they lose their appetites."

"I'm for that," Gloria said, "but we have to at least offer some *token* food."

"There's cheese in the fridge. It's covered in blue fur. It's having babies."

"Scrape off the fur," Gloria said. "There are some Triscuits in the cupboard above the sink."

"They've been there since September 11, 2001."

"Why do you remember that?"

"I bought them to eat while watching CNN all day, and now, whenever I look at Triscuits, I get that sick-for-the-fate-of-the-world feeling."

Gloria nibbled a corner of one. "They're soft. I'll broil them and make them crispy again."

Steve resuscitated the cheese while Gloria began broiling up the stale Triscuits. The couple was having what other people might call fun, but then Steve cut his finger. "Aw, *shit*."

"You're bleeding all over the cheese."

"Where are the Band-Aids?"

"In the drawer below the phone."

Steve opened the drawer and found Band-Aids and a box of liqueur chocolates. "How long have these been here?"

"Since three Christmases ago."

He bandaged his hand and then peeled the foil from the chocolates and ate five in a row before Gloria shrieked, "Don't eat them! We can serve them to our guests."

"Dessert?"

"Exactly."

Steve sat down and stared at the phone. In his head, he was pretending he had super powers and could magically make the phone ring. It didn't.

Steve was always looking out the window and up at the sky for planes—he liked to think he could stare at a plane and will it into exploding before his eyes. They never did. The only thing that made the endless departmental meetings bearable was that, from his seat, he could watch the flight path to the airport, and on a clear day could practise his pyrokinesis while his underlings schemed and backstabbed. He didn't know it, but when he put on his "pyrokinesis face," he looked wise and handsome. It was this illusion of wisdom and virility that kept his underlings from mutiny. Steve never made the connection that on clear days his staff were much better behaved and agreeable than on cloudy days.

"Goddam hot water spout!" shouted Gloria.

Steve woke up from his reverie. "What about it?"

"It's not powerful enough to blast your blood from the nooks and cracks in the cheese. And now the cheese is starting to get squishy."

Steve turned the faucet to cold. "Rinse it quickly, then let's put it in the freezer for a few minutes. When it comes out, we can scrape away the squishy outer layer of cheese, and the bloody bits with it." Steve flared his nostrils. "I think the Triscuits are done. We have barely enough cheese to cover them."

Gloria felt a harp's gentle glissando of love for her husband. It swelled from nowhere; it was unexpected. She decided not to battle for the next five minutes. "I think I'll change gears from Scotch to gin," she said.

"You do that, baby. Hey, check it out—we've got pickles in the fridge door shelf—two of them. There's our vegetable. I think we've nailed all four food groups."

Bethany

I love *Glove Pond*.

Steve and Gloria's lives are so small. I can't believe how small life can become. I sit on the bus and the world becomes as small as the dot at the end of this sentence. And then I wake up, as if from a spell, and look out the windows and see that while I've been obsessing about how my mother threw out my old cosmetics, the rest of the human race has been out there designing microchips and collecting money for orphans in faraway lands.

I think I need to see more of the world. I've only ever been to Seattle twice, and Banff once. Last year I went to see this lame death-metal band over in Victoria, but Victoria doesn't count. Europe's been on my mind lately. I go online and concoct dream tours of London and Paris, which is a total escapist girly thing to do, and it's kind of embarrassing—but I want to go somewhere some day!

God, it's reached the point where I look at my shadow, and it feels like a ball and chain anchoring me to this stupid store in this stupid suburb in this stupid new century. My question of the day is, "What if my shadow became unattached from my body? What if one day I went one way and it went the other?" Wouldn't that be strange— if my shadow moved off to some other place and began leading a separate life—if it got its own apartment and a job? Maybe it'd shack up with those hitchhiking souls who've left their owners' bodies. Maybe they'd have a way better time than they ever did being stuck to us. We'd try to instigate legal proceedings to make them come back to us, but no way, José.

Today's big news is that I swiped a pack of Wrigley's Orbit White chewing gum from the rack up front and then spent the morning chewing every piece, one by one, placing the resulting gum wads underneath the Bic Soft-Grip display racks. Talk about life on the edge. And let's be brutally honest here: can gum *actually* whiten your teeth? Kyle's teeth used to be yellow. That was before you started working at Shtooples. And then one week we all noticed his teeth were bleached paper white, and instead of everybody razzing him, they all went out and got white teeth too.

Sheepy-weepies.

Does anybody have off-white teeth these days?

Oh, and before lunch these two gay guys came in to buy price stickers for their garage sale, and they went for the expensive ones with little strings and grommetted string holes. I got their address because if they take that much care, they probably have some pretty good stuff.

Back to you.

Who's Joan? And even if you've had fifty jobs, you seem like you could do better than working here. And you mentioned a car crash way back. Who was in it? What happened? Funny how I can ask you these questions on paper but not to your face. BTW, it's fun pretending I don't know all this stuff about you. Are you getting off on it as well? Let's keep it this way. It keeps life interesting.

Five minutes later: Kayla came in and asked me the strangest question. She wanted to know if it was true that tomatoes grow at night. I said, "*What?*" But she said that tomatoes are members of the nightshade family, and one of their main characteristics is nighttime growth. I asked why she was asking *me* this, and she said, "Well, you act and dress like you're totally into death, and nightshade *is* a poison, and all that."

"You asked me this because I wear black lipstick?" I said.

"Pretty much."

I told her to google it.

Ten minutes later: Just back from the PC aisle. I couldn't wait for Kayla—the idea of being able to generate nutrients without needing sunlight was too exciting not to immediately investigate. Alas, I couldn't find the answer online, but now I'm determined to make a garden out of plants that only function in the dark.

It's so quiet here in the staff room right now—I like being in here alone. I can only concentrate when things are totally quiet, like being in a forest with no people. I did that growing up—I hiked into the watershed for miles so that I couldn't hear anything man-made. It was so perfect. I look back now and can't believe I didn't end up as cougar chow.

But I'm thinking about what you said right at the start of all of this—about people wanting out of their lives, even if their lives look great from the outside. I saw this picture in a magazine of this family in some flooded place down in the South. There they were, up on their roof, having a barbecue and waving and smiling for the camera crew in the helicopter. It was like they got a Get Out of Jail Free coupon and had change imposed on them rather than having to change themselves.

Blairzilla just walked in. Break over.

Pretend you're me again.

Roger

A few years back I had to organize my son Brendan's funeral. Joan was completely wrecked, and I was barely keeping it together. I remember sitting there with the funeral director, trying to think of what to say in the death notice or whom I could invite to speak. I drew a blank, and the director, an older guy—white hair, a head shaped like a stone dug out of a Scottish field, a guy who'd been through a trench or two—suggested that no one had to speak and we could recite grade school stuff like the Lord's Prayer. He said that most people know it by heart, and we could all get through the proceedings with a sliver of dignity.

He must have smelled my breath—tequila—because he looked at me a moment, then went to his desk and pulled out some very peaty Scotch, almost like soil syrup, and poured both of us a few fingers. He told me that most people who come to arrange services don't believe in anything. He said that if he's learned anything from doing his job, it's that if you don't have a spiritual practice in place when times are good, you can't expect to suddenly develop one during a moment of crisis. He said we're told by TV and movies and *Reader's Digest* that a crisis will trigger massive personal change—and that those big changes will make the pain worthwhile. But from what he could see, big change almost never happens. People simply feel lost. They have no idea what to say or do or feel or think. They become messes and tend to remain messes. Having a few default hymns and prayers at least makes the lack of crisis-born insight bearable. The man was a true shepherd of souls. Why don't men like him run for public office?

The car crash. Okay. It was the early eighties and we were in two cars: Jeff was ahead of me driving his ex-stepfather's hotwired Cutlass. He was with Corrine, Laszlo and Heather. I was following in my Monza 2+2.

Jeff was this low-life I met during my one month in community college. He may have been a low-life, but he was an amusing low-life and you could always count on him to do something, anything, to enliven a day, even if it meant throwing a milk bottle out his fifth-floor-apartment window while seated in a beanbag chair by the TV, not having a clue what the bottle would hit. He could shock you. We got high on mushrooms and walked through Stanley Park one summer, and he began breaking the flowers off roses and evergreen magnolias and used the petals to write the word E-N-E-M-A in six-foot-high script outside the park's central cafeteria windows, where all these families with their kids were staring at him. Then he had a screaming contest with a peacock. Ever heard the lungs on those things?

That night we were all baked on weed and we'd been having a group hug in the parking lot of the Fraser Arms when I suggested that Laszlo drive, not Jeff. That was all it took to set Jeff off. Suddenly, I was a jerk and a bring-down, and then I was in my Monza by myself, gunning the engine to keep up with the others—no one had told me the address of the next party. It was raining, and they went off a bridge into the river between the airport and Richmond. The last thing I saw was the car going down quick, Corrine banging the rear passenger window, looking me in the eye. The interior lights were on. And then the car was too deep to be seen. And then there was just water, like the dawn of time.

That's how quickly things happen in cars. They shatter time. They destroy it. The car sinking took fifteen seconds, but it's stretched for nearly twenty-five years.

The fortune-telling lady was right: I did change my ways for a little while after the accident. But I got lazy, and also, other things changed. I'll leave it at that for now.

Glove Pond

Steve decided to take an interest in dusting. To this end, he pulled a cut-up pair of Y-front underwear from the rag drawer and a can of lemon Pledge from under the sink. He went into the living room on his quest, and he was richly rewarded.

"Jesus, Gloria, have you looked on top of the piano lately? You could shoot pool here. There's so much dust it's like a goddam billiard felt."

"People are starving in Africa and you fret about dust?" Gloria said. "I hate dusting. Worrying about dust is so middle class."

"I saw a show on TV." Steve was inspecting the piano's top at eye level. "It was all about dust. A layer of dust is like an ecosystem. It has burrowing creatures and organisms that live on top of it. It decomposes and mulches itself, and that attracts more organisms. Dust is ninety percent dead skin."

"Steve, you're making me sick. Put that rag away. Don't upset the dust. It's happy the way it is."

"This place is a dump, Gloria."

"Steve, we used to be able to afford a maid."

"Yeah, well, we used to own tech stock."

"We've been through this a thousand times. I'm not

going to become a parlourmaid because Pets.com went south. One needs to have standards. First I'm dusting—and before you know it, I'm out selling matches on street corners. Sit down and have a drink."

"I think I will."

Steve and Gloria drank in silence—silence that Steve shortly broke. "Let's have a few of those cheese and crackers. I'm hungry."

"Me too."

"But only a few. We have to save some for the guests."

"Right."

Within minutes, all the cheese and crackers were gone, and Gloria had eaten the two pickles. Now what would they feed their guests? Steve remembered some pancake mix at the rear of the cupboard. Was the mix beweeviled? *That's okay. Heat will kill them.*

Roger

Some basic info: My name is Roger Thorpe, and I'm the oldest Staples ~~inmate~~ employee by a fair margin. I'd divide the staff into two groups: the no-hopers (serial twelve-steppers and the terminally clueless) and the kids who are making a quick pit stop before they head off to something real. I read in a newspaper last week about this scientist who claims that the human race will, over the upcoming millennia, split into two distinct species. One will be a superhuman race, the other, Gollum-like hunch-backed retards. His argument is that selective breeding will produce an underclass that will then become a distinct race. Scientists have already isolated part of our DNA that "intelligent," "sociable" types have and others don't. I think these scientists should come into Staples and do some DNA swabbing. I think we've already leapt into that future and the rest of humanity needs to catch up with us.

Me? I like to flatter myself that I represent some form of third option, the invisible forty-three-year-old man.

I like the fact that I'm invisible to my co-workers.

Strike that.

It *kills* me that I'm invisible to them. The fact that they don't see me means that I'm truly old, and it's hard to grow old in a place—a city—where everything is so young. Being old means no sex. Being old means never being flirted with. Being old means that Shawn and Kelli make spooked eyes at each other when I come in from my smoke break and grunt a hello in their direction.

Psycho!

I miss sex. Once upon a time I could take off my shirt and walk down by the beach carrying a Frisbee and there wasn't a girl there I couldn't confidently chat up. That was my prop, by the way, the Frisbee. Couldn't toss one worth a damn, but people see you holding one of those things and in their minds you're suddenly this well-balanced person who's never had gonorrhea or police issues—and you can probably summon a well-groomed, cheerfully dispositioned golden Lab with a single whistle.

Last month I plotted out how I'd win the attention of these junior shits here who speak and think like chimps. I was going to work my butt off, totally kiss ass with the regional boss and thus win Employee of the Month. Imagine the no-hopers coming in and seeing my picture on the little wall plaque. Dear God, it might actually give them hope. *Hey! If Roger can do it, then I can do it!*

I don't know why I work here ~~in hell~~ at Staples and not someplace else. Bethany here is confronting me on this issue, and I don't know what to say. I've had so many real-world jobs—in offices where people have their own parking spaces, and where biweekly meetings are held, and where they have Christmas parties. I drank my way out of all of them. Pre-Internet, I could get away with it. These days, if you type "lush" into Google, I would likely be the first hit.

Fucking Internet. I can't even move to someplace

remote where they still speak English, like Tasmania or South Africa. They'll know my dirt.

They.

So until I figure out an escape clause, it's Staples for me. It's okay in its own way. It demands little of me and I demand little of it. I like being rude to customers. I like starting to serve them and then vanishing for a smoke break for fifteen minutes. They always ask for the supervisor, Clive, but Clive knows that I'm here for a longer haul than the younger workers, so he doesn't discipline me. Even on the days where I get hosed on vodka and stack cartons of twenty-pound bond all day, not a shred of discipline. Hah!

Discipline me.

Master! Master! Beat me!

I'm an adult. Discipline me and I'll bury you alive.

Roger as Bethany

I'm Bethany.

Did you find everything you were looking for today?

That's this dorky phrase I have to say every time I ring in a sale, even to kids. It'd be great, for once, if somebody looked me in the eye and said, "Well, I wrote the word 'Fuck' on a piece of paper in the felt pen section, and then I drew an anarchy symbol, and then I stopped thinking or breathing or anything, and I had this experience where time stopped and I wasn't on this planet any more—like I was sucked out of myself—and I didn't have to care about the world or people or pollution, and instead all I had to do was be in awe of the stars and the colours and the effort that went into making the universe safe and warm like a womb. And then I snapped out of it and I was staring at the Crayola boutique and the moment was gone. After that, I walked around the aisles like I'd been clubbed. I was going to steal the felt pens instead of paying for them, but I'll steal them some other day. Right now I'm still in the afterglow of experiencing the universe. And you ask me, did I find everything I was looking for today?"

I have to wear this red shirt at work. We all do. It's like scientists got together and selected the one colour from all the known colours in the universe that makes everybody's skin look bad. In any other shirt, I look white as a ghost. When I put one of these things on, my skin pinks up like a strawberry milkshake—my mouth is a black olive.

Shtooples lighting was selected by the same scientists who chose the shirt colour. It possesses strange powers. For example, if you have blackheads, as Rudee does, this lighting actually *amplifies* them. If you have other blemishes, this lighting acts as a lens to make them larger and far more apparent. At least we people who work here know this and can cover up the worst of things with concealer. One of the few joys of this job is seeing how bad some customers look when ambushed by the lighting system. We're like a species of beige toads.

Roger's skin is okay, but only barely. It's all that booze he soaks up. And he's the world's worst shaver. Women have to spend half their lives indignantly shaving hair off legs and armpits, while guys only have to shave their faces—how hard can it be?

It's weird shaving your legs when you're not in a relationship, or there's not even a possibility of becoming close to someone. Who's going to see me? My mother, I suppose. Did I mention that I'm in my twenties and still living at home? Yes, that is correct, I am a loser.

Here's something weird: Roger went to high school with my mother. That's how old both of them are. I wonder if they jointly won the yearbook award for Most Likely to End Up in Depressing Lifestyles?

Oh God, I just imagined the two of them on a date, at some generic place like Denny's, and they're both trying to be nice to each other, and they're both trying to figure out how much booze they can order, and how quickly, without looking like lushes. And then they stare at the menus—the laminated ones where all the food in the photos is pumped on steroids and sweating nervously, like it's lying to you. My mother knows that if she eats one and a half pounds of food, she will gain one and a half pounds; she has no metabolism. She's trying to see if she can order only a celery stick, and then realizes she can order a Bloody Mary with a celery stick, so she's happy. Roger picks up on this momentary happiness and uses this little happy window to order a double rum and coke. The two of them are practically dancing like Snoopy in their orange banquette seats.

But then they have to make conversation and the mood vanishes. They talk about where their old friends are—divorces, money woes, surprise careers, the odd death—and they both feel sadness not simply for themselves but for the planet. They feel sad because life is over so soon. They feel sad because they've blown it. They feel sad because they have to order food, except suddenly the photos on the menu aren't food any more. They're dead animals and chunks of starch. The two of them aren't vegetarian, but they're off meat for the time being.

But back to me.

I had a thought today—not an original thought, but it's better than no thought at all. Wouldn't it be great if stars turned black during the day—the sky covered with dots like pepper?

Bethany (for real)

Thanks for being me again, Roger. Does my mouth really look like a black olive? My mouth is too small. I hate it.

It's weird to describe how it feels, walking around the store knowing that you're walking around these same aisles imagining your way into me—like being possessed—the sensation that there's a ghost or something slipping in and out of my body whenever it wants. I don't mind it. It's what people probably felt like all the time before TV and the Internet. People probably tried harder to get inside each other's heads in the old days.

So *you're* that guy my mom dated last year. She came home piss drunk and howling like she'd lost her favourite piece of jewellery. You took her on a date to *Denny's*? That's so recovering alkie. What were you *thinking*?

She can't help but admire my frugality?

Hubba hubba! Sexy, Roger!

For that matter, what was my mother like in high school? Was she always angry? Was she the goody-goody she always pretends she was? If I saw her at seventeen, would I be able to imagine the way she turned out? Pink eyeballs. Sno-Kone cellulite. Mood swings like a Slinky pulsing between left and right hands.

Last New Year's we both sat on the TV room carpet and finished a bottle of Kahlúa while we figured out how much time and money it would cost her to get a total surgical makeover, from the daunting English ivy varicose veins on her calves right up to silencing her forehead with botox. The full meal deal came to $80,000, which actually doesn't seem that expensive for a whole new everything in life: teeth, eyes, skin, nose, cheeks, chin, hairline, boobs, stomach, hips, thighs and knees.

Oh, and she'd have to go to the gym, stop smoking and start eating food that doesn't come in cans or boxes. And she'd have to meet people out in the real world doing real-world things like dog walking and swimming and line dancing. And in order to afford it, she'd have to sell or mortgage the condo, and I think she should. She needs escape velocity if she's ever going to get out of her present life and into a new one.

But let's talk about you. Maybe you're not a total alkie, but booze does explain things about you. Let's face it, Roger, you're a disaster. I thank my biological father for teaching me all about that alkie shit before he flaked off with Cerise when I was a kid.

Maybe I should try being you on paper for a while. I'll think about it. It's actually a fucked-up thing to do, trying to stick yourself into somebody else's head. I've never done it before, though I did this pathetic two-year stint at a local community college that shall go unnamed, and I had to take an English course in creative writing—it was hippie stuff like, "Pretend you're a piece of toast being buttered. Write it from the toast's point of view." All I remember from the course is everybody almost going insane having to wait until it was their turn to read their stuff out loud. And when people started reading their stuff, it was like they were taking the class hostage. It didn't matter what slop people wrote, everybody had to be nicey-nicey to them afterwards. I don't think anybody learned a thing, and I don't think you missed a thing by not finishing college.

You're really good at pretending I don't exist here in the store.

What happens next in *Glove Pond*?

PS: You nailed my feelings about having to say *Did you find everything you were looking for?* I have this fear of being seventy and having a stroke, and the only thing I'm able to say is, *Did you find everything you were looking for?* Shoot me if that happens.

Glove Pond

Steve sat in the living room, waiting for the doorbell to ring. Gloria was upstairs changing her lipstick colour. Steve stared at his five critically successful, financially disastrous leather-bound novels, third shelf up in his walnut bookshelves, a wedding present from Gloria's family. Being head of an English department in a large university was no salve for the source of his pain: his lack of fame and the fact that he had to have a day job. He thought it odd to be so successful yet not successful at all.

He looked at the top of the piano, where a swath of polished wood shone through a cloak of dead skin cells and burrowing micro-organisms.

When will the doorbell ring?

Using the same part of the brain he used to try to make jets explode, Steve willed the doorbell to ring.

It didn't ring.

Steve thought about how hard life was as director of the English department of a large, prestigious university. He was exhausted from being a pit bull, always protecting the English language within his faculty, guarding it from a never-ending onslaught of change. The English language was noble to Steve. It should never ever, ever, ever, ever change, no matter what. If Steve could have his way, English would have been frozen with Henry James. 1898? Somewhere near then. Steve rather daringly thought of Henry James as his favourite writer because James defined the cut-off point after which the English language was never to be permitted to shift. Steve wondered if his faculty members had ever trashed him behind his back for his daring taste. Maybe he should opt for Poe. Poe died in 1849, while James, dying in the twentieth century, had a taint of modernity about him.

Steve also felt sorry for Poe because of something that had happened on the way home when he'd stopped to buy some pens at an internationally franchised office supply megastore—a colossal exercise in horror and bad taste. After drifting through a dozen aisles—assaulted by endless cardboard pop-up point-of-purchase displays and totally ignored by the churlish deaf, dumb and blind children who ran the place—he finally found the pen aisle. Of course, the small pieces of paper people use to test out new pens were littered with FUCKS and SHITS and satanic emblems.

Then he heard two young women behind him restocking the CliffsNotes. One of them said to the other, "*Tales of Mystery and Imagination* was okay for someone who had the misfortune of being trapped in the nineteenth century. Back then, the range of metaphors was pretty limited. The only high technology they had was staircases. And windows. Windows were as high-tech in 1849 as nanotechnology is now."

"Poor Poe."

"I know. What he needed was a PlayStation and some Zyban."

The doorbell continued not ringing.

Steve was drunk and decided to shift perspectives—now he could care less about the language. The sooner it was destroyed by geeks, mathematicians and TV producers, the better.

All the English language has ever netted me is five novels that never sold and a wife who worships literature the way deep-sea insects are drawn to the glow-in-the-dark dangling thingy that hangs in front of an ultra-deep-sea angler fish.

Steve took another sip of Scotch, which at last turned off the buzzing part of his brain. All that remained was the realization that his own written words were generic. They could have emerged from any creative writing workshop in North America in the late twentieth century. Hell, his words could have emerged from a creative writing program taught at the Department of Motor Vehicles. The critical praise he'd received—it wasn't real. It was from people who merely needed to suck up to him. Poor Gloria—she wickedly resented his feeble book sales. She hated the way she and Steve consistently failed to garner dinner invitations from people in other cities who might somehow drag them out of their appalling yet prestigious university town.

Poor Gloria. She might as well be wearing a ball and chain, the way her husband's failure has tethered her to this shithole.

Wait . . . can a ball and chain tether a person to a hole? Well, whatever.

More staring at the front door.

More willing the bell to ring.

Gloria called from upstairs, "Is the doorbell broken?"

Roger

I'd run into Bethany's mother, DeeDee, one afternoon around two o'clock. It was last year, a few months after Joan left me and maybe ten minutes after I realized she wasn't coming back. I was in Aisle 5-North, restocking highlighter pens, and DeeDee asked me where she could take her toner cartridge for recycling. She asked without looking at me—which is pretty insulting and oh so common. I knew it was DeeDee Twain from high school, so instead of ignoring her as I would have done with other people, I told her I'd show her the recycling bin but first she'd have to fondle each of my butt cheeks. To see her face! When she realized it was me, she smiled and swatted me with her purse, and it was sweet, like we were both cutting class. I seized the moment and asked her out to dinner.

It started out well—a few drinks and each of us blowing off steam about our jobs. Halfway through the meal, she was drunk enough to be lighting the wrong end of her cigarette, but not drunk enough to become indignant when told that smoking in the restaurant wasn't allowed.

Of course, we discussed changes in our lives and the world. In particular, we discussed all of the ugly houses and apartment buildings that had been built here in the city in our lifetime. Back when I was young, I told her, I assumed that within my lifetime they'd all be quickly demolished and replaced by something newer and better. "Imagine all of our dumb, ugly, contractor-built little houses standing there long after we're gone."

"You're being depressing, Roger."

"All they'll ever do is draw attention to our narrowness of ambition and vision."

"I'm ordering another drink."

DeeDee changed the topic and told me that her condominium's co-op board was on her case for keeping a cat. I said I didn't see why cats were such a big deal, but she told me it wasn't the actual cat that was the problem; it was the $600 plumbing bill to snake out the clots of kitty litter choked inside the bathroom pipes. She confessed that this had happened not once, but twice.

You have to remember that two years ago my freefall had just begun. I'm used to it now, but it was all very fresh then. A chronology of my life would read:

Thorpe, Roger
- Wife's cancer diagnosis: 2003
- Totally cancer'ed out: 2004
- Seeks diversion as stagehand in local theatre production of Neil Simon's *Same Time Next Year*: 2004
- Canned from desk job at insurance firm: 2004
- Makes one stupid mistake he pays for the rest of his life: 2004
- Dumped by embittered wife: 2004
- Learns the disturbing financial cost of anything legal: 2004
- Old friends pretend not to notice him in a checkout line: 2004
- Rents basement suite from condescending yuppies: 2004
- Seborrhea inside hairline: 2004

- Begins work at Staples: 2005
- Ugly phone calls with Joan: 2004, 2005, 2006
- Unable to afford Halloween candy, so he sits in basement apartment with all the lights off: 2004, 2005, 2006
- Weekend highlight: learning how to use a photocopier's collating function: 2005

I was hypnotized by the speed of my life's implosion, but DeeDee was having no truck with my self-pity. She said, "Guys forget that women have to make their peace with their half-assed lives too, and earlier than men. Women get more realistic far faster than men do, so don't expect tears in your beer from me, Roger. To me, you're a rookie at this failing life shit."

I reached over to touch her hand, and she yanked it back.

"I want to go home."

"But . . ."

"Roger, I feel so . . . *old*."

"Tonight was supposed to be about making you feel young again."

She slid a twenty under her water glass. "Nothing about the past ever makes me feel young."

I watched through the window as she got into her car and drove away. I got sloshed.

Glove Pond

Gloria was in her boudoir—a delirious vision of a 1930s Hollywood set director, pushed to the farthest, pinkest extreme. Not a hard surface existed anywhere in the room. What was not carpeted was covered in velour or velvet or starbursts of ostrich and marabou feathers. The room smelled of violets and tuberoses, breezeless and claustrophobic, as though heaps of rotting blossoms were concealed behind drapes and beneath the divan.

Gloria was trying to decide which colour she would try on her lips, but the sound of the doorbell not ringing was driving her crazy.

She reached down to touch her spleen, which was puffy and irritable. Fortunately, she'd paid attention during her Vassar biology lessons and knew that a spleen is a ductless gland not strictly necessary for life, and which is closely associated with the circulatory system, where it functions in the destruction of old red blood cells and the removal of other debris from the bloodstream.

A puffy spleen—what could that mean?

She looked at her artillery of lipsticks. She remembered how her mother always used to throw out all her old makeup and how it drove Gloria crazy. As an adult, she overcompensated by never throwing out anything. Steve once told her that her makeup table resembled the road tour makeup kit for the entire cast of *Cats*. To punish him, Gloria withheld sex for several months.

Falling Blossom Pink. Perfect.

She looked for some Kleenex to blot the previous colour from her lips, but realized she had run out. All that remained were some used sheets hastily stuffed into her dresser drawer the previous spring—long enough ago that any microbes they once harboured would have disintegrated, thus making them reasonably safe to use again. So she blotted her lips, sipped a gin and tonic, and wondered about the evening's guests—an academic and his wife. This young chap had recently published a novel that was selling countless copies and was receiving wonderful reviews. He was handsome, and his wife was good-looking. Steve's nerves were in ribbons over his very existence, let alone his imminent arrival in their home. Gloria was going to savour every minute of it.

She looked at the Kleenex box. *Is the plural Kleenices? I do love words and writing and art and music.*

The doorbell continued to not ring.

Silence disturbed Gloria because of something she had once heard on PBS. Apparently, the first thing a baby hears upon being born is silence. It's spent its entire life prior to that surrounded by heartbeats and valves gushing and liquids sloshing to and fro. And then, suddenly, it's born into a new world, deprived of everything its ears have ever known. Who invented that?

Babies . . .

Children . . .

No time to think of that now.

She looked at herself in the mirror and pursed her Falling Blossom Pink lips. *I could easily be Elizabeth Taylor, circa 1972, approximately three weeks after abandoning a strict diet.*

The doorbell rang.

Bethany

Okay, Roger, here's my deal.

My best friend in grade four was Becky Garnett. She didn't show up for school one day, and within a month she was gone from this freaky stomach cancer that prepubescent girls get. Dead? I was used to people vanishing, to people going out for cigarettes and never returning, but *not* to people dying. *Becky?*

After Becky came this five-year death fiesta. Both my grandfathers in the same year (car crash; kidney failure); my twenty-year-old stepsister (internal injuries sustained in an assault by her now behind-bars-for-thirty-years ex); my grandmother (emphysema); my favourite music teacher, Mr. Van Buren (car crash on the 99, driving up to Whistler); Kurt Cobain; both my cats (Ginger and Snowbelle); two of my smokehole friends, Chris and Mark, who smoked some pot cut with PCP and were found waterlogged two days later in the lagoon beside the sand traps at the local pitch-and-putt; my stepbrother, Devon (hanged himself); and then my eerily, disturbingly, relentlessly perky Aunt Paulette. She had lightning-onset breast cancer, and all the money we raised doing car washes to send her to the Revlon Center in Los Angeles didn't work, and she wobbled away into nothingness—no drama, only silence.

At the end of all of this death, death, death, I began to find myself dreaming about all of these dead people at night—pretty much to the exclusion of living people. It scared me that I was spending so much time with dead people, and then I realized this was snobbery. Why should only living people count in your dreams, while dead people get relegated to "filler" status, unable to be taken seriously? Imagine the dreams of a thirty-year-old living a century ago. There couldn't have been a living soul in their dreams. I think we forget that growing old is as much an invention as electricity or birth control pills. Long lives aren't natural. God or Whoever didn't want millions of ninetysomethings hanging around forever, and if he did, there had to be a reason beyond simply staying alive for the sake of staying alive.

Me? I expect people to die soon. Dying is what people do in my universe—I'm a statistical freak. Most young people don't know a single person who's died. I'm a throwback.

Last week, Kyle wanted to know if I worshipped the devil or something like that, and I wanted to blow him off, but then I realized maybe he was worried about something, so I calmed down and asked him how things were going. Turns out his grandmother died and he doesn't know how to deal with it. What you were saying about not having faith in place when things go bad—well, there's your proof. I asked him what he thought the afterlife might be like, and I got the impression that he thinks death is like a resort where everything is pre-decided for you and all you have to do is lie back and submit to the regime.

I disagree.

Much of the time I want to be dead. It must be nice to be dead, to know that the sheer work of having to constantly learn lesson after lesson is over and you can coast for a while. I think our souls are totally rigged for this.

Here's something that happened to me last summer. I was visiting Katie in the house beside our condo building—the Divorcée Who Got the House—and she'd installed a fish pond where the barbecue used to be. Katie, despite her bimbo demeanour, is tough as nails, and smart. She said, "A pond needs to be an ecosystem, and it has to be able to take care of itself in case I have to fly to Cabo for a week or something." So she had these jumbo snails put into the pond to balance the ecosystem. I'd never spent much time looking at snails, so I lay down on my stomach and put my head close to the water's surface and looked deep into the water—it was dark but not too dark, like decaf coffee—and I saw the snails sliming their way over rocks and across the pond's rounded concrete bottom.

And that was that.

And then, for the next five nights, I had snail dreams—snails crawling over everything—not in a gross way but in a natural "that's what snails do" way.

I mention this because in total I've watched maybe five years of TV in my life and I don't remember once having a TV dream, and yet I look at snails for five minutes and I'm having snail dreams all over the place.

So I guess the point is that our brains are rigged to respond to what's natural, not what's man-made. Snails will always win over sitcoms. And the dead will always win over the living.

And that's why I am the way I am. It's why I shun the

sun, wear my black lipstick and don't give a shit if my weight exceeds norms established by the government.

And guess who got reprimanded for the dust all over the cardboard mechanical pen display? Yes, that's correct, me, even though it was technically Shawn's job to fix it.

My voice is shot today—a cold or flu—and it sounds so damaged, but I like the sound of damage. It's like Patty and Selma from *The Simpsons*.

I love *Glove Pond* more than ever.

Hey—again, what happened with your family?

Roger

I'm sitting in my car in the parking lot, and the weather is changing outside; the sky's going from dry, crazy thrashing in all directions to something slow and wet, and my eyes are wet, and where did that come from?

My Hyundai got keyed this afternoon, and I know who did it. I didn't get their licence plate number because I was too busy cutting them off in traffic. I guess they followed me to the lot here at work, which is all to say that I deserved it, but at the same time I'd like to kill the bastard. My Hyundai is—*was*—the only unflawed thing in my life. I'm actually more sad than I am pissed.

No, I could kill.

Death.

Life always kills you in the end, but first it prevents

you from getting what you want. I'm so tired of never getting what I want. Or of getting it with a monkey paw curse attached. All those Hollywood people are always saying to be careful what you wish for, yeah, but at least they first had a wish come true.

Hang on, I'm venting here.

One more breath.

I imagine myself sitting in a glade surrounded by woodland creatures that rest on my arms and shoulders, sleeping, utterly comforted by existence.

Breathe once more.

Who am I fooling? I merely did whatever everyone else seemed to be doing. It'd be nice if we had a course in school called Real Life. Forget don't-drink-and-drive videos and plastic models of the uterus. Imagine a class where they sit you down and spell everything out, deploying all of that information delivered to us by our ever-growing army of wise, surviving ninetysomethings . . .

. . . Falling out of love happens as quickly as falling in.

. . . Good-looking people with strong, fluoridated teeth get things handed to them on platters.

. . . Animals spend time with you only if you feed them.

. . . People armed with shopping carts who know what they want and where they're going will always cream clueless people standing in the middle of aisles holding vague shopping lists.

. . . Time speeds up in a terrifying manner in your mid-thirties.

My Theory of the Day is that the moment your brain locks into its permanent age, *whoosh*, it flips a time switch and your life zooms forward like a Japanese bullet train.

Or the Road Runner. Or a 747. The point being that your soul is left behind in a cloud of dust.

And all of those dead people in your life. I dream about Brendan every so often, but when he was alive, I never dreamed about him. Ever. How sick. When he was a toddler, I remember worrying about the fact that I never dreamed about him. If someone's big in your life, you dream about them. Is their absence from your dreams disloyal? Is it cheating? I dream about my old high school locker twice a week. I dream about our old next-door neighbour's poodle—dead twenty years now—twice a month, and I'm sure if I stared at snails, they'd become a nightly feature with me.

The thing about dreaming about dead people is that you don't know they're dead—your brain makes you forget that one key fact. And then you wake up and remember they're dead, and you feel the loss all over again, every single time. You feel scooped out and hollow. I do. It's been three years now. Hit by a car while he was riding his bike. It was instant. Joan couldn't handle her Brendan dreams. Unlike me, she'd been dreaming about him since the moment she knew she was pregnant. Her counsellor kept trying to tell Joan that she should look at Brendan's dream visits as something wonderful, treasures to remember him by. That's when Joan stopped going to see the counsellor and went on autopilot taking care of Zoë. And then she was diagnosed with spleen cancer and she never really changed gears along the way, and the two years wore us ragged and we never recovered. Or, rather, I didn't—I *think* Joan did. Who knows? I don't think anyone ever gets over anything in life. They merely get used to it.

"You answer the door."

"No, *you* answer the door."

As their guests waited on the other side, no doubt bored as well as chilled by gusts of arctic air whooshing in to refrigerate the fall evening, Steve and Gloria bickered.

"Why should I?" Gloria was indignant. "*You* heard the doorbell first."

"We both heard it at the same time."

"That's not true. I was upstairs, so technically you heard it first."

"No, I didn't," Steve said. "The doorbell's ring mechanism is directly beneath your makeup collection, and as sound travels more quickly through solids, chances are that *you* heard the doorbell ring first. And tell me, your Grace, why *won't* you answer the door?"

"Because it's my role to be walking down the stairs in a gracious manner while you answer the door. That way, I can work on my character of Lady Windermere too. My devotion, my dear, is to my craft. And, tit-for-tat, why won't *you* open the door?"

Steve was matter of fact: "I think it befits the

director of a highly prestigious English faculty to be seated near the fireplace when his guests arrive, perhaps holding a snifter of highly exclusive brandy."

"Let me get this straight," said Gloria. "You'd put your petty vanity ahead of my need to be an artist?"

"Tell me, Gloria, does Lady Windermere actually descend a staircase in the play?"

Checkmate. "No."

Steve felt he could already taste Gloria's opening of the door. Then a voice inside his head said, *Wait—can one actually taste the opening of a door?*

Gloria, however, surprised him. "Steve—if I agree to discuss your five novels with you, would you consent to opening the door?"

It had been years since they had discussed his five critically acclaimed yet poorly selling novels. "Maybe." He was wary.

"Is that a yes?"

He chewed the lower knuckle of his right index finger. "Yes."

Gloria climbed the stairs to position herself.

"Not so quickly, Meryl Streep. You agreed to discuss my five novels."

Gloria shrugged. "Very well, then. Shall we go in chronological order?"

"Please."

"Okay, novel number one, *Infinity's Passion.*"

Steve's face bore the expression of a kindergartner just moments before the commencement of an Easter egg hunt. "Yes?"

"Potent but impotent. A cuckold's vagina."

Steve protested, "What the hell does *that* mean? *Infinity's Passion* established my career. Without *Infinity's Passion*, how would we have been able to live in a stately home built of Connecticut slate, with a steep staircase that allows you to descend to the front door like a hostess from another, more gracious era?"

"Novel number two: *Less Than Fewer*. Forced. Anticlimactic. Emotionally arid and repetitive."

"Nonsense. Critics compared it to Henry James."

"Yes," taunted Gloria. "If I remember correctly, an *embalmed* Henry James—inasmuch as words can be embalmed."

"Jesus, Gloria," shouted Steve. "Why do you have to be so caustic?"

"Novel number three: *Gumdrops, Lilies and Forceps*."

"That was a good book!"

"Yes, well, whatever. Novel number four—*Eagles and Seagulls*—the story of my family, which you pilfered as easily as if it were a pack of gum."

"Not true. Merely because its heroine has copper-tinted kiss-curls like your mother's does not mean I strip-mined your family for material."

"If you need to believe that, then please do. Let's discuss novel number five, *Immigrant Living in a Small Town*, which began your final decline into the creation of meaningless compost mounds of spew."

Steve removed his hand from the door handle. "How dare you! *The Times Literary Review* called it a masterpiece of miniaturization. 'A Five-Year Plan of the Microscopic.'"

"What have you written lately, my dear?"

"Oh, for God's sake, is it that important to you that I be the one to answer the door?"

"Yes, it is."

The doorbell rang again.

They looked at the door as though it were a coffin, with two bony claws about to crash through in pursuit of living souls upon which to feed.

"You know I've had writer's block for a long time, Gloria."

"Open the door, Steve."

"Yes, dear."

Steve did.

DeeDee

I don't understand the human heart.

Only pain makes it grow stronger. Only sorrow makes it kind. Contentment makes it wither, and joy seems to build walls around it. The heart is perverse, and it is cruel. I hate the heart and it seems to hate me.

Roger, you stay away from my daughter. She tells me you've been writing letters or something back and forth. Well, put a stop to that right now. She could be the only member to escape the curse of my loser family, and I won't have you stepping in and setting her on the road to failure. Bethany has not had an easy life, and much of that is my fault, and somehow she's managed to rise above it. She lives at home and is the only thing that keeps me going. I dread the day she leaves, because once she's out that door, I'm out the door too, except my body is left behind, here in this crummy condo, forever wondering what it was that walked out the door with Bethany.

She was a quiet child, and I used to think it was because she was smart and had ideas too large to put into words, but now I think she kept quiet to avoid having to engage in her mother's sordid life.

After she leaves, I'll have way too much time on my hands and will have no choice but to accept the fact that the chance of my falling in love again is zero. When did I reach that point? A few years ago?

I know the moment I finally understood it. It was that night at Denny's with you. It was like I saw myself at the next booth, sixty-eight years old, eating breakfast alone at three in the afternoon, using a coupon for a discount, with the only thing on my horizon going back to my condo to wait for my next meal.

So it's not like I haven't been thinking of you since that date. But when I do, I think about The Void. About loss. You may or may not deserve this, but that's what I see. You may well be the male equivalent of me—a certain age, a grocery list of bad decisions—whatever. Stay away from my daughter. She has a nice healthy thing maybe going with some guy there—Kyle?—and I don't want you messing with that. Act your age. Go get hammered at some bar. But leave my daughter alone.

DD

Gloria smiled at her guests. "Kyle Falconcrest! An honour to have you here in our charming, gracious home."

"Thank you. This is my wife, Brittany."

"Hello."

Steve said, "I'm glad you could take the time to visit our small, modest university. Can I get either of you a drink?"

The young couple looked at each other. Brittany said, "Do you have any white wine?"

"All we have is Scotch. Would you like some Scotch? No wait—we have some gin, too."

Gloria's eyes widened; she would never surrender her private stock. Steve recanted: "No, just Scotch."

Kyle said, "Scotch is fine. On the rocks, please."

"We're out of ice cubes."

"Neat."

Steve went to fetch the drinks, and Gloria ushered Kyle and Brittany into the living room. "Kyle, your novel is magnificent."

"Thank you."

"I read it twice. It deserves all the acclaim it gets, and the huge royalty cheques you receive must sweeten life too."

Kyle blushed. Brittany said, "He's just today signed a second book deal."

Gloria veritably shrieked, half to her guests and half towards the kitchen, "A second book deal! How exciting! I can only imagine how much money it was for."

Brittany said, "It hits the papers tomorrow, so it won't be much of a surprise then. Ten million dollars."

Gloria almost fainted with pleasure. "Ten million dollars?" She called to Steve, coming in from the kitchen. "Young Kyle here is getting $10 million for his second novel."

"Is he?" It was the most Steve could do not to break a highball glass on the table edge and slit his own throat. "Let's have a drink, then."

He passed his guests their glasses and Gloria immediately proposed a toast: "To your $10 million book deal."

Steve had no choice but to join in the clinking of glasses.

"What is your new novel about?" Gloria asked.

"It's a modern love story with a twist."

"A twist? How thrilling."

"It's about people who work in an office superstore."

"An office superstore?" Gloria was confused.

Steve, using the tone of voice adults use when proving to younger people that they know the current hip bands, said, "I was in one today, as a matter of fact. Staples."

"You didn't tell me that." Gloria felt betrayed.

Brittany volunteered a description. "They're those huge box stores near the freeway off-ramps. They're everywhere. Staples, Office Depot. Those kinds of places."

Gloria took on the aspect of someone trying to attach a name to a face at a party. "I . . ."

Steve said, "For God's sake, Gloria, everyone knows about office superstores."

"I buy my stationery at that store a few blocks from here. It never occurred to me to go to a . . . an office . . . *superstore*."

"You can get tremendous deals at superstores," said Brittany. "Post-it Notes and reams of bond paper are half the price they are at smaller, non-globalized stores. The aisles are wide. You can shop in comfort and style. They even have entire aisles devoted solely to ballpoint pens."

Gloria felt out of it. "Tomorrow I'm going to make a point of visiting an office superstore."

Steve felt like he'd won a small victory, but the smirk on Kyle's face robbed him of joy. "How's your drink?" Steve asked.

"It's fine. I have to go slow on the booze and watch my diet if I'm going to meet my deadline."

Gloria purred to Kyle, "It must be something to be young, handsome, rich and talented, with a beautiful wife and the future wide open to you. Don't you think so, Steve?"

Steve replied by fetching more Scotch.

"What are you working on now, Steve?" Kyle asked.

"A new novel."

"Really?"

"It doesn't have a title yet."

Gloria said, "Actually, the book doesn't exist yet."

"That's not true," Steve said. "I'm well into it."

"What's this novel about, then?"

"Curiously, it also takes place in an office super-store."

"What a coincidence!" said Brittany.

Gloria sniggered.

Kyle was confused. "Really—an office superstore? You're setting a novel in an office superstore? Are you far along with it?" Kyle asked.

"Oh, you know, a few chapters."

"Well, I'll be—"

Gloria said, "Steve, why don't you give us a reading?"

"I couldn't possibly do that, Gloria. The book is too young to be released into the world."

"I see."

Brittany asked, "Do you spend much time in office superstores, Steve? By the way, I must confess, I'm a fan of your work. *Gumdrops, Lilies and Forceps* was deeply moving. It changed the way I view fertility in literature." She blushed. "I can't believe I actually get to call one of my all-time heroes 'Steve'—in his own house, no less."

Gloria blurted out, "I'm an actress."

"Oh?" said Brittany, taken by surprise.

"I'm Lady Windermere in the local theatre produc-tion of *Lady Windermere's Fan*."

"Isn't that something," said Kyle.

"For me it's all about the craft, you know. Act, act, act."

Steve quickly batted the conversation back on track: "I go to office superstores all the time. I enjoy the wide array of goods they provide at reasonable prices. And they're such a—you know—a popular phenomenon. I think it's important to *engage with society*."

Kyle sipped his Scotch. Was Steve *really* writing a novel set in an office superstore? As far as Kyle knew, Steve's concept of literature was frozen in time roughly three weeks before the invention of the telephone.

Steve said to Kyle, "I'm so busy at the university I haven't had time to read your first novel. Tell me, what is it called?"

"It's called *Two Lost Decades*."

"A good title."

"Thank you."

"What's it about? A vulgar little question, but in the end, it's the only one that matters."

"Okay. Because you ask. It's about this guy. He's fortyish. He used to be married, and had two kids, but one of them was hit by a car while riding his bike. Almost immediately after that his wife got cancer, and at the beginning it brought his family together in a way that he had never imagined possible, but that didn't last long, and a fog of death clouded their lives for a year. Then his wife got better, but she was tired, and our protagonist was tired—and he'd also said and done foolish things during the fog—so his wife left him, getting custody of the child.

"This guy endures all of these tribulations, except they don't change him. They don't make him a better person. They make him a worse person. He begins to lead a falling-down life. His body won't fit his old clothes, and he doesn't know how to find new ones. He keeps waiting for the moral of his life to appear, but it never does. The clock is ticking, and all he can see is decades more of the same thing until his body gives out, and he wonders what the point is of being alive if it's merely more of the same—and the thing is, he'd *like* to change things, but he doesn't know what, or how. He sees a scam in everything the world offers. He doesn't believe in the Apocalypse, and he thinks that both faith and reason are equally stupid, and that all leaders are frauds.

"He tries to lose himself in work, but he's also lazy. He wonders if he should declare himself a ward of the state and live in a homeless shelter, but he can't bring himself to do that, though he feels close to the edge. He looks back on his early life for clues to his present disaster, but he doesn't think he was raised to be overly dependent on others or without morality or without a few practical hints for good living. But the other people in his family are pretty tight with each other, and he knows that on those rare occasions when they discuss him, or even think about him, it's probably not too fondly or with much charity. He used up all of his 'welcome coupons' in the family department when he was younger. He pretty much used up his welcome coupons *every*where. He feels wretched, yet he knows that he has a ways to go before he hits bottom. Perversely, a vision of the bottom keeps him going. Every morning he's curious to see what new indignity he will be subjected to— what flagrant new assaults will be made on his good taste. And will he ever change in some way that's good or meaningful?"

There was a pregnant silence after Kyle's plot summation. Steve used this moment to try to remember the office superstore he'd visited that very day, that grotesque hangar filled with Chinese-made office crap, staffed with kindergarten students and offering all the charm of an airport luggage-handling facility. *Steve, you can write a novel set in an office superstore. You can. Bring a notepad. Pretend you're an anthropologist—anthropologists can do anything and appear smart. Who knows—perhaps a grand theme will emerge from the stacks of underpriced CDs, vinyl attaché cases and software upgrade kits.*

Steve realized the silence was going on a bit too long (oh yes, that wretched young man's wretched novel) and looked out of the corner of his eye at his wife, her jewelled talons clasped to her bosom, her eyes tearing up. "So deep. So truly, *truly* deep," she said, casting a taunting eye at Steve. "So simple and yet I felt blood pulsing through every fibre of its being. Intelligent, yet broad. And it's sold millions of copies, correct?"

"Ten," said Kyle. He then looked at Steve's bookcases. "Steve, are those leather-bound copies of your five novels I see there?"

Bethany

I should be mad at my mother for writing to you, Roger, but I'm not because that's exactly the sort of depressing thing she does—not only writing a paper letter during the golden age of email, but also *mailing* it to you with a *stamp*. At *work*. What kind of person gets mail at work?

To hear my mother speak, you'd think her life was something shattered and gone, like Superman's home planet. But she's got friends, her job, *and* when I leave home she'll still have me in her life.

I dream of going to Europe one day. What exactly is it about Europe? People go there and suddenly all of their problems are solved, and as a bonus they're suddenly sophisticated and glam when they come back. *Hello, I'm Count Chocula. Welcome to my chateau. We'll dine on peacock livers atop little pieces of toast cut into triangles with the crusts removed. After that, I'll ravage you with an heirloom jewel-encrusted dildo from the Crusades, and then we'll discuss the socially beneficial effects of government-sanctioned drug injection sites.*

Listen to me; I can barely wait to find out.

On *my* pay? Ha.

So . . . *Kyle*. Ever since he talked about death with me, something clicked and I have to say I really kind of like the guy. I know he's dumb as five planks (he can't remember the PLU number for gum), but this afternoon he brought me a CD of songs containing the word "moon." He's cute, and he doesn't find me repulsive, and he's not gay, so why not go for it? My mother makes it sound like we're engaged in a Mormon courting ritual. *Gee, Kyle, before we go to A&W, let me fetch my Holly Hobby prairie sunbonnet so that other men don't lust for me against their wills.* He's just a nice guy.

As for you . . .

I don't know how to begin addressing all the issues in your life, Roger, but I do find it interesting that the hero of Kyle Falconcrest's first novel doesn't believe in the Apocalypse. That's wrong. How could you possibly be alive and on earth and have a set of eyes and ears and a brain and not figure out that some kind of end is near? It's in the tap water. It's in the freshness-sealed pound of bacon you bought last week. It pulsates in the air every time Blair's cellphone rings with her lame 1980s retro Madonna "Holiday" ring tone.

The end is near.

I think about it all the time—how the end is going to look and feel. When it finally happens, it won't be the way I thought it would be. Here's how the end of the world happens: It's a Sunday afternoon, and I'm at a barbecue in someone's back yard. I'm sick of too many people and of standing in the sun for too long, so I go around to the side of the house and sit in an old folding chair, wishing it were nighttime and that I hadn't come to the party. I'm looking at a fly buzzing in front of me. It isn't bugging me or anything—I'm tracing its flight pattern in the air behind it, like an invisible waggling strand of yarn, when out of the blue, the fly stops and falls to the ground.

And the world becomes quiet: the voices around the corner near the barbecue stop, as does a touch football game—but I can hear the hamburger patties chattering on the grill. But a neighbour's weed whacker two yards over stops, as does someone's lawnmower.

I know right away what has happened—every living thing on earth except me has died. People, seagulls, earthworms, bacteria and plants. I look at the trees and shrubs and think, *Well, of course they're not brown yet, they've only died just now—but they're not trees and shrubs any more—they're more like giant cut flowers in vases. In seven days, they'll be brown like everything else.*

Everyone at the barbecue simply *stopped* where they were. It isn't gruesome or anything. Their eyes are open.

Then I start hearing thumps and explosions from all over the city—cars wiping out, planes crashing, incinerators and furnaces exploding like popcorn on the back element—at first just a few, and then more and more. And then they stop, and I begin seeing streams of smoke reaching up into the sky, like shoestrings, binding the planet to the universe—so many smoke streams and clouds.

I look at my feet and see a dead barn swallow. I see bumblebee carcasses all over the patio. I go inside and pick up the phone—it's dead too. I see a bowl of cut dahlias on the counter, and for a moment I think that's ironic.

And then I start to feel unwell. Know what it is? All of the organisms in my body that aren't "me" have died too. Those happy bacteria that live in the stomach, good viruses and bad viruses and symbiotic amoebas and all that small, scary shit—dead. Your body isn't just a body, is it? It's an ecosystem. And my body can't handle all of this dead stuff floating around in it.

So I go out onto the patio and sit down on a chaise and stare up at the sun. It's warm out, and I feel happy to be joining everyone else wherever it is that they've all gone. People never mention that as the upside of death, do they? It makes your own death less scary to figure you're going to meet up again with old friends!

Where was I? Oh yeah—sitting on the chaise, staring at the sun, growing weaker and weaker. Finally, as much as I hate the damn thing and its endless, droning, perky lightness, I enter it.

Glove Pond: Kyle

Kyle Falconcrest remembered his first day on the job in the office superstore, the fateful job that led to his grand insight that he should set his second novel in such a place. He was almost thirty, old enough that at night he'd begun dreaming that he'd be working a crappy day job forever. He saw no escape. Kyle had made the mistake of thinking that working in a bookstore or a place where office supplies were sold would bring him closer to the throbbing pulse of modern literature. To Kyle, literature was a place of experimentation—a laboratory, an art gallery where exciting new ideas never, ever, ever, ever stopped.

He remembered his first day on the job, being assigned his first aisle: Tape, Fasteners, Correction Fluids, Pens, Pencils and Markers. He was told that if he did well, after a year or so he would be promoted and Aisle 5A would be added to his territory: Art Supplies, Educational Supplies, Scissors and Rigid Art Boards.

Kyle never got used to the office superstore. Although it was brightly lit and sterile, he couldn't help but look at the endless truckloads of toner cartridges and flash cards and protractors and laser printers and imagine how they would all end up either mummified inside a regional landfill, or incinerated, the ashes floating about the Van Allen radiation belt, soaking up extra heat from the sun and hastening the total meltdown of the polar ice caps. To Kyle, the office superstore was a slow-motion end of the world in progress. You had to look at the place, squint, and pretend you were watching stop-frame animation in which the camera snapped a photo only once a month. Seasons would come and go. The winters would get warmer and warmer, the ground ever more covered in soot. The number of animals and birds crossing the parking lot would dwindle. The grasses and shrubs near the entrance/exit would wither and then, after a few decades, the road headed west, away from the store, would vanish as the ocean rose. And yet people would still be buying presentation portfolio covers, extension cords, Bankers Boxes and, on impulse, gum.

Kyle considered all of this as he stared at Steve, who was blathering on to Brittany about that quintet of doorstops he called his novels. They were neither trendy nor timeless nor contemporary nor passé. Steve's novels inhabited some parallel time stream where time didn't exist. To find one of Steve's novels in a second-hand store was to experience the same sort of lump in the chest one feels when reading in the paper about a baby being smothered by parents on crack. *Poor little thing.* And yet Brittany was twirling the ends of her hair like a cheerleader flirting with a jock. Kyle found it shocking that he could love someone who was a fan of Steve's novels, let alone be married to her. Liking or disliking Steve's work should be a mating pre-selection factor on par with heterosexuality and homosexuality. In this one way, Brittany truly baffled him.

He glanced at Gloria, who was wearing the pleasant, tuned-out expression used by presidential wives during dinner speeches and idly fondling her spleen.

"When is dinner?" he asked.

As Kyle Falconcrest asked his semi-rude question about dinner's readiness, Gloria was thinking about lipsticks. She was thinking about the massive industrial base that had to exist in order for her to purchase a single tube of Ruby Tuesday at the town's sole remaining non-Wal-Martized department store, a doomed and dispirited brick heap not far from her stationery dealer. Lipstick makers had to secretly kill thousands of whales without Greenpeace looking on, and then they had to flense the blubber from the carcass and stuff it into zinc canisters to ship to her favourite cosmeticians' factories. The blubber then had to be boiled into bacteria-free goo, at which point a staggering amount of pigment and stabilizers and texturizers had to be added, after which the coloured muck had to be solidified, inserted into chromed flexi-rods, vacuum sealed into a perverse amount of packaging, and then trucked out into the world along complex interstate freeway systems and rail lines, their voyages heralded by massive print and electronic ad campaigns that made the world's Glorias bay with desire.

What if everybody on earth suddenly turned stupid? What if we couldn't make lipstick or anything else? That would be the end of the world, wouldn't it? What if everybody's IQ simultaneously dropped fifty points? For the first hour or so, nobody would notice, but then it would become obvious. *Hey—who forgot to turn off the nuclear power plant? Boy, this fuel tanker sure is hard to navigate through these rocky bodies of water. Does anybody here remember how to work this fire ladder? I'm sorry, kids, I was going to make wiener schnitzel for dinner, but I forgot the recipe, and besides, the butcher couldn't slice any veal because the machine jammed and nobody knows how to fix it.*

From there it would be only a brief amount of time before the planet "cracked open like an egg," a line she remembered from an old *Planet of the Apes* movie.

Oh humanity!

How tenuous is our plight!

Gloria delivered those made-up lines in her mind as though they were lines in a play—a play starring Gloria. This, in turn, reminded her of her inability to remember her lines as Lady Windermere, a shortcoming that was bringing her fellow cast members close to mutiny. *People, how can I bring Lady Windermere to life if you don't give me time to fully express myself?*

Leonard had taken her aside. "My frisky little schnitzel, you have until Monday to get your lines straight. Yes, I enjoy banging you as much as the next guy, but there's only so long I can cover for you. Take some B vitamins, lock yourself in a motel room and learn your frigging lines."

Philistine.

Gloria does not require vitamins to memorize her lines.

She idly fondled her spleen. *Why would a spleen suddenly become puffy and inflamed? How unusual. I'm sure it's nothing serious.*

And what about dinner for young Kyle and Brittany? Not to worry. They're young. They don't need much nutrition. They could live on their body fat alone for weeks. Gloria then waxed nostalgic for the recent past: *My, those last few pickles really were tasty. I should buy some more some day.*

In the end, it was easier simply to ignore Kyle's question.

Glove Pond

As Steve described in loving detail to Brittany the birth pangs of each of his five novels, a part of his brain was wondering if Kyle thought he was stupid. Kyle had that look Steve sometimes saw in his more challenging students. What pains in the butt they could be. He much preferred the students who showed up, asked if they would be graded on attendance and then sat like drugged houseplants for the remainder of the semester. The Kyle Falconcrests of this world were trouble— young Kyle certainly wasn't paying a respectful amount of attention to Steve's loving dissertations. If anything, Kyle was watching Gloria massage her spleen.

Steve's stomach growled.

Time for more booze.

But Brittany was leaning towards him expectantly, twiddling her hair, and so he continued talking. He finished discussing water metaphors in *Gumdrops*, *Lilies and Forceps*, and was about to take on *Less Than Fewer*, when a chill rippled down his spine and he had a vision of the end of the world that froze him to his core. In his vision, everybody on earth suddenly became a genius.

Brrrrrr . . .

Imagine a world populated by back-seat drivers, a planet where everybody knew the answer to everything, and where everybody was out to use their new genius to grab more for themselves. Everybody would find secret shortcuts to get home from the office, thus clogging all the streets. At the grocers, newly minted food experts would select only the finest and freshest fruits and cuts of meat, placing undue strain on the food industry. Everybody would invest cleverly in the stock market, but because everybody would make millions, all of the world's currencies would collapse, and banking would come to an end. The world's bauxite miners, banana pickers and assembly line workers would rebel against their soul-deadening jobs, and would begin roaming the world's streets in pursuit of knowledge. Since geniuses don't make food, starvation would become rampant. Dazzlingly intelligent hordes would invade neighbourhood after neighbourhood, flushing out caches of freeze-dried astronaut food and tinned goods.

Throughout this rapid decline, billions of newly minted book readers, in between pangs of starvation, would pick up a copy of any of Steve's five novels, read them and find them lacking. And it would be young Kyle Falconcrest, in between his time spent translating Chaucer into Mandarin and developing a perpetual motion device, who would cast the first stone.

And to think Kyle expected Steve to feed him!

Roger

DeeDee, I'm not trying to lure your kid into my car with a pile of candy or something, so lay off, okay? She can make up her own mind about things. And thanks for thinking of me as Mister Cosmic Fucking Nothingness. That makes me feel good.

Since when did you get so negative, eh? You were a sweet kid in high school—not stuck up, ever. And for what it's worth, I remember the week your body blossomed. Man, it happened so quickly with you. Trust me, it's the sort of thing guys notice. All of the guys in our grade did. You were a peach, and I remember wanting so badly to stroke your cheeks in social studies in ninth grade. You sat by the alarm bell, and for two weeks in spring, the sun came around and haloed your face during the last class of the day. It was like you were made of something insanely delicate, like dandelion fluff, and anything harsher than a gentle breath would destroy you.

Do you remember high school? I don't. I dream about it every now and then, but only things like opening my locker or missing a big test—all that symbolic stuff. I try to recreate a sample day from back then, and I blank out.

Do you remember how you felt at seventeen? I do and I don't. I remember being outgoing and probably smooth with the ladies. But . . . imagine you came from outer space and someone showed you a butterfly and a caterpillar. Would you ever put the two of them together? That's me and my memories.

Or maybe memories are like karaoke—where you realize up on the stage, with all those lyrics scrawling across the screen's bottom, and with everybody clapping at you, that you didn't know even half the lyrics to your all-time favourite song. Only afterwards, when someone else is up on stage humiliating themselves amid the clapping and laughing, do you realize that what you liked most about your favourite song was precisely your ignorance of its full meaning—and you read more into it than maybe existed in the first place. I think it's better to not know the lyrics to your life.

Do you ever wonder what the old gang remembers when they hear your name? More than anything, DeeDee, I bet people would remember your face the moment you got dumped in the dunk tank during the school fair, when the strap came off your Cheerios bikini and you blushed the colour of cherry cough syrup. It was totally funny and not sexy, nipple and all.

Bethany has had a lot of people go away on her, and so have you. People leave in so many different ways. People go nuts. They abandon you. They stop liking you. They get lost in their own worlds and they never come back. Or they simply give up. And yes, they die.

DeeDee, cut me some slack. I'm not a void, and I'm not a monster. Bethany is a muse. I thought muses were a stupid concept from the past, but they're not. She helps me write, and I don't know why. Because of her, I was able to start my first novel, and it's going amazingly well. You never know—it could be a really successful book that sells a lot of copies, and it could be my ticket out of this hole I'm in. I'll show it to you when I can—it's a bit raw right now. You know how it is with revisions—you work so hard to really *nail* the exact word or phrase. You don't want things coming out sounding pretentious and unnatural.

Please relax, DeeDee.

Your scribe,
R.

Bethany

Hey, Roger, I saw you throwing a tennis ball to Wayne this morning. I was on the bus, and you were in the park down by Mosquito Creek. It was raining, but it didn't bug you— you looked happy, actually. So I thought I could borrow a bit of your happiness today. I need it. It's One of Those Days.

Earlier on there was this guy in line who was nice enough—buying one of those black office chairs—and the signature was worn off his Visa card, so I asked him if he had a driver's licence for ID and he went apeshit about how I didn't trust him and how nobody trusts anybody these days. So I told him I didn't want to lose my job because Visa only gives card users a strip of glossy white ink-repellent plastic that's one-eighth of an inch wide on which to write a signature that rubs off after two days inside a normal wallet or purse. Whatever. In the end, I had the law on my side—as well as the manager—but I got bummed about people not trusting people.

When I turned sixteen, my mom told me, "Bethany, there's a difference between intimacy and closeness." I asked her what she meant, and she said (I paraphrase), "You'll meet a stranger in an airport bar, get shit-faced and tell them things about yourself and your life that you'd never *dream* of telling anybody you actually knew. But does that make you *close* to that person, Bethany?" From the way she went on about this, I got the distinct impression that La DeeDee has been spending time in airport bars.

I wish I had a dog like Wayne. I wish I didn't make fun of stuff so much. I wish North Korea didn't have nuclear weapons. They're nuts. Days like today get me thinking more about the end of the world. I look back on when I was younger, back in the 1990s, and how naive and goofy everything was back then, but it was like this happy bubble, a time snack, a little patch of bliss before the shitstorm.

There's such a difference between the world I grew up expecting and the one I got, but everyone my age has probably felt the same since the dawn of man. I didn't expect a world full of jetliners impregnating office towers, or viruses jumping species or, shit, according to Yahoo!, pigs that now glow in the dark. The modern world is devoted to vanishing species, vanishing weather and vanishing capacity for wonder. The few animals that remain here with us—when they look at me, or when I hear them cheep or bleat or meow—they're not animals anymore, they're the voices of the dead trying to warn us of what's coming. According to government statistics, I'm supposed to leave the world in 2062, but I can't even see 2032 in my head.

Change of subject:

Wayne's one of those dogs that smile. And I see he likes to fetch things. I divide dogs into two categories—those for whom you drop a stick and they look at it like it was a rock, and those who pick even rocks up and who like to chase and fetch things. I think Wayne would jump off a cliff for you.

Now that I think about it, dammit, I want a dog.

Five minutes later:

Kyle gave me a sandwich-sized Ziploc bag full of trail mix, heavy on the almonds. We're having these really great discussions about mortality because of him losing his grandmother. I'm kind of scaring myself at what a pro I am on the subject, but he really needs me. I get the feeling he's never actually had a *real* conversation with anybody before.

The hospital freaked him out the most. He went to visit his grandmother in the extended-care ward in a private room, and because of the tangled mess that is his father and his collection of trophy wives, Kyle ended up alone in the room with his grandmother most of the time. She was on a respirator and morphine and totally out of it, and he tried to relax and look at the snow that was just beginning to dust the mountains, and—here's the funny part—he'd try to use psychic powers to make planes crash, just like Steve!

Another change of subject:

Blair got fired for stealing gum. They got it on tape.

I hate the future.

PS:

QUESTION: What did DeeDee have for breakfast this morning?

ANSWER: Several cigarettes.

Glove Pond

An hour melted away as Steve lectured his guests about his five novels. He smiled at Brittany. "Do you know what *The Boston Globe* said about my fifth novel? They called it 'A Five-Year Plan of Miniaturization.'"

"Oh my."

Steve then realized it might be a good idea if one of his guests had a chance to speak . . . *Perhaps that young Falconcrest chap would like to say something.* But then Steve remembered that Kyle was a writer and would most likely want to discuss his own writing: *bor-rrrrrring.* Steve groaned inwardly, looked at Kyle and realized that, as a host, he had no choice but to ask his guests about their opinions and ideas. He jumped off the cliff: "Tell me, Kyle, you must enjoy reading as well as writing. What books have been important to you and your life?"

Kyle looked at his host, and Steve thought he looked almost stunned.

"Really? You're asking someone a question? I'm shocked."

"Nonsense. You're a guest in my home, and you're also a fellow writer. Writers as a group are always giving, unjealous and supportive of all other writers. Nothing makes a writer happier than hearing of another writer's success—or hearing another writer discuss his or her books. So please, Kyle, do tell us what books have shaped you and your life."

"Well . . ."

Kyle began to speak, and as he did, Steve tried hard to give the illusion of listening. His mind drifted off to other moments in his life when he'd asked writers the same question. They invariably chose something by that upstart monster Salinger—a one-trick-pony almost pitifully dependent on telephones for his plot lines.

What other books did writers like? Oh yes—pornographic stewed cabbage by that pederast . . . what was his name—Nebulov? Nunavut? Nabokov? Yes, Nabokov—and his book *Lolita*—the masturbatory rantings of a deviant perpetuating his unclean, lustful ideas.

As Kyle continued to speak about whatever it was he was speaking about, Steve's mind drifted back to an incident involving the novel *Lolita*—an afternoon a decade before, at the university, when a crazed den of love-starved lesbians from the Women's Studies Department had organized a seminar dedicated to removing *Lolita* from the school's reading lists. Steve had entered the room by accident, to avoid another professor approaching from down the hall. The Women's Studies ringleader, upon seeing Steve at the back of the room, asked for his view on the book, and Steve said it was pure filth.

"Did you read it when it first came out, or have you read it recently?"

"Read it? I've never read the thing."

"Let me get this straight," said the woman. "Here,

in a university, you're denigrating a book you haven't actually read?"

Steve mumbled something about papers in need of marking and quickly bolted.

. . . Blink!

Steve emerged from his brief academic reverie and was once again in his living room. *Oh God, I asked this Falconcrest fellow his opinion. Now I have to actually listen to it. Okay, Steve, brace yourself. Open your ears . . .*

Kyle was saying, "I guess I'd have to say that I have trouble believing in the future, and I think the past is largely an embarrassment. In general, I don't trust people. There's very little to believe in, and all I've ever been able to believe in are a few cherished books by a few people who I suspect feel life is as fleeting and ghastly and cruel as I do. I think Truman Capote's *Answered Prayers* documents this sensibility as it occurred in a variety of long-vanished, almost mythically privileged cliques. I admire Joan Didion's *Slouching Towards Bethlehem* and *The White Album*, and pretty much everything by Kurt Vonnegut testifies to the wretchedness of life, with an occasional sunbeam sent along to brighten things up."

Who are these writers he's speaking about? Steve's mind again drifted off, and he tried to remember who was sitting beside whom at the previous day's intramural Dewey Decimal System workshop. Something as simple as the wrong seating plan could undo decades of political work, and since the introduction of stacking chairs in the eighties—after much bitter and angry debate—meetings had never been the same.

Falconcrest prattled on.

"I guess I like work that examines unexpected crisis points in modernism. Sherwood Anderson's *Winesburg, Ohio* examines the collision between rural and industrial life in the early twentieth century. Bret Ellis's *Less Than Zero* chronicles the implosion of secular middle-class values in pre-digital California. Chuck Palahniuk's *Fight Club* is a brilliant assault on consumer culture, while everything J.G. Ballard has written can't but make us rethink the path our world is taking—particularly *Running Wild*, a book that makes me wonder if the only hope for our world is to spawn children who have mutated so far beyond our present selves that anything we have to offer them as a survival tool is pointless and quaint."

Steve was mentally day-planning the upcoming week: a dozen meetings, perhaps write a letter pleading for an advance from his publisher for a book he'd been on the cusp of starting for—how long was it now?—fifteen years? twenty? Maybe a trip to the liquor store and, if he was lucky, the delivery of a black-and-white photo magazine from San Bernardino, California, dedicated to the healthfulness of unclothed sun worship.

Steve once again tuned in to Kyle's words . . .

"To be honest, I'll read anything, even the four-point warnings on pharmaceutical packages—I like looking at the lines on product bar codes and pretending I can judge which number a line represents from its comparative thickness against the others."

"Bar codes?" Gloria was puzzled.

Kyle continued, "I think that every reader on earth has a list of cherished books as unique as their fingerprints. I'm always kind of suspicious of young people who, when asked who their favourite writer is, say Henry James or someone equally as dead. Imagine if you asked a young person who their favourite musician was and they told you Vivaldi. Would you trust that person? I think that, as you age, you tend to gravitate towards the classics, but those aren't the books that give you the same sort of hope for the world that a cherished book does."

Steve looked across the table and noticed a mosquito-like insect landing on the Scotch bottle's snout.

"You know," said Kyle, "I wish, I really, truly wish, Steve, that people were honest with you when they were asked which books influenced them. I think that a lack of honesty about this one question is the shame of the literary world. I ask you, which books held a light for you in the darkness?"

Brittany looked at Steve. "Kyle's given that same speech twenty times this year."

Kyle smiled. "But I still mean it."

"You could at least stop trying to pretend it's the first time you're doing it every time you do it."

"What are you getting at?"

"Kyle, right now you've given that same speech twenty times already. But in twenty years you'll have told it thousands of times . . . won't you have? Doesn't that exhaust you in advance . . . knowing that you'll one day become this anecdote robot?"

"How sweet!" said Gloria. "A spat between a writer and his wife. *Look* at them, Steve—aren't they darling? They remind me so much of you and me back when we first started out."

Roger

I like booze.

Booze makes me feel the way being in a womb must feel. If fetuses aren't getting alcohol, what *are* they getting in there that makes the womb everybody's dream vacation spot? I bet they're floating around and getting wasted on fet-ohol. Imagine the withdrawal newborns must go through when their supply of fet-ohol leaves their bodies and their nervous system's alarm bells go off: *Hey! You're part of the world now!* Brutal.

I think scientists should be trying more than anything to find the formula for fet-ohol. Imagine taking a hit of "F": "The Security Drug"—you'd feel like you were safe and happy, even if you were doing boring everyday crap like collecting spray-painted shopping carts from the ditch across the road by the Indian reserve or haggling with some pathetic senior trying to scam an extra twenty percent off the purchase of a Maxell CD twelve-pack using an expired coupon.

But then, fet-ohol would probably have some backfiring aspect. That predictable monkey's paw: official key fob of Saint Teresa of Avila, patron saint of the answered prayer. If you became a fetus again, you'd become autistic or a zombie, or would pull so far away from the world that people looking at you would think you were a vegetable. Fet-ohol would convert your brain back into the brain of a fetus. It wouldn't be the same thing as brain damage—instead, your brain would sort of erase itself, like a CD or a tape. You'd be unborn.

Why do I mention any of this? Because of my mother.

Years ago, I visited my parents' place on a Saturday afternoon. My dad was downstairs, my mother upstairs. My dad and I said hi, and then he called upstairs, "Honey, your favourite son is here for a visit!" and my mother came downstairs, almost skipping like a girl. "Chris, I've made your favourite peanut butter and raisin cookies," she called, and then she saw it was me and the temperature dropped to zilch. "Oh. Hello."

"Hi to you, too, Mom."

She stared at me, and—okay, it's not like I haven't done enough shit to merit a frosty reception—but this time was different. She seemed afraid of me, definitely something new, and after a few seconds of locked eyeballs, I realized that something new *was* going on here. She didn't recognize me.

My mother's Alzheimer's was more rapid than that of most people with the disease, and it struck her in her late fifties, which is rare but by no means unheard of. One week she couldn't find her car keys. A month later the police phoned to say she'd been found cowering in the women's bathroom outside the Bay cafeteria and had no idea who she was.

When Mom started wetting herself and that kind of thing, Dad had to get a live-in helper, Dolores, to help out. Dolores was Mexican and treated Mom like a child, which Mom definitely seemed to prefer to being treated like an adult. Six years after it all began, Dad divorced Mom and married Dolores, and by the time Zoë came along my mother was completely gone. She died of pneumonia a month after Zoë's birth, and I really have to wonder why we went to all the effort to keep her going. Were we cruel to elongate her time on earth? Was her life enhanced? Did she suffer—especially on those nights when she'd start hollering and screaming and we couldn't figure out why? And is the world a better place for her having gone through it all?

The thing with Alzheimer's is that the patient and everybody in their life knows all too well what's happening; the walking-on-eggshells factor is remarkable. Simple lapses such as forgetting a phone number create tension like a storm's about to break, which triggers denial, which often triggers fights and tears. In a weird way, only when the disease is in full expression is there any form of relief. A sufferer forgets who he or she is, and where he or she is—everything. What do they dream of at night? Do they dream the dreams of a fetus? Are they back on fet-ohol?

Bethany

Roger, the funniest moment in my short history in this dump of a store happened this afternoon, and you missed it. This middle-aged guy totally lost it in line. Kyle was at the till, and, well, let's face it: God never intended for Kyle to be working at a till. He was meant for other things. But anyway, this guy comes in—forty-five? Dockers. Dorky sage green checkered short-sleeved sports shirt, like something a left-wing politician would wear to a golf course—and after waiting in line for a while he starts shouting, "You incompetent brats. For God's sake, if you're a fuckup at your job, either quit or get fired. But don't ask me to subsidize your uselessness with my good will. I am not here to be your learning curve. I am here to pay for my purchase without having to watch you learn new product code numbers every single time you ring in an item."

Kyle was unfazed by this—he's got psychic Teflon. So he kept on plugging away in pursuit of correct code numbers until he found the right one.

I was taking down the Halloween displays by the window. Shawn whispered to me, "That's Mr. Rant. He's nuts. He hasn't been in for ages. He can actually be fun if you get him going." So I figured, what the hell, and I asked the guy, "Is there anything else that annoys you, sir—I mean, while we're on the subject and all?"

And he totally got into it. "Potato skins," he said. "I *hate* them. They're ugly, they taste shitty, and let me dispel one pernicious myth right now: not only are there no vitamins or minerals in them, they're supermagnets for pesticides, fungicides, larvicides and other agrochemical residues. Restaurants that serve unpeeled potatoes are too fucking lazy to peel them. End of story. Potato skins are pure laziness crystallized into earthly form, and if you want science to back this up, check out recently skyrocketing cancer rates in the intensive potato farming areas of Prince Edward Island."

I said, "I know exactly what you mean. Potato peels taste awful, and people always try to make you feel bad about yourself if you don't do a little happy dance when they put them in front of you."

"Finally, someone else who cares."

"What else bugs you?"

"Since you ask, I actively dislike people who refuse to own a microwave oven out of a misguided notion of moral or biological superiority. Come on, who the hell do you think you're impressing? Every time you use a conventional oven, you're sucking trillions of wasted megawatts from the national power grid. Microwaves are smart, efficient and good for the planet. And thanks to China, they're almost free with a tank of gas these days. What the fuck is with that country? How do they manage to make shit even cheaper than it is already?"

"Everything in this store is made in China," I said. "If I think about it too much, I get a queasy feeling. What else bugs you?"

"Why do restaurants heat your plate before they put your food on it? There always has to be some asshole with a blow torch in the prep area, scorching the crockery in a warming oven, thus ensuring that when your food arrives in front of you, it will emit too much steam and generate blackheads. Your server will say, 'Mind the hot plate,' and then, after waiting ten minutes for the thing to cool down, when you finally do take a bite you burn your tongue or the roof of your mouth. The whole hot food thing is a scam. Humans were meant to eat food no hotter than the temperature of blood."

"Amen."

By now, Mr. Rant was next at the till. I looked at the item he wanted to purchase and said, "I like Sharpies."

Mr. Rant began talking to his twelve-pack of pens: "How did society ever function without you, little Sharpies? Your nibs have the precise amount of give to create a line quality with character, yet not so much character as to be smushy. Thank you, little pens."

I told Kyle the product code number, Mr. Rant bought his pens, and then he was gone.

What a freak, but he made my day.

Roger, I've never known anybody with Alzheimer's. Can you tell if *you're* going to get it? Also, how did you learn so much about books and writers and writing? I thought you didn't finish college. I am in awe.

Speaking of school, I'm thinking of going back. You'll shit, but I think I might like to be a nurse. Thinking of Kyle alone in that room with his dying grandmother flipped a switch inside me. What do you think?

Before I forget, the other night I told my mother that we were still exchanging words and she said, "You know, maybe Roger's not the ogre I made him out to be."

I will never understand that woman.

B.

Glove Pond: Brittany

It was hard for Brittany to be both a respected surgeon and the wife of literary sensation Kyle Falconcrest. This evening was a perfect example. Neither of her hosts had, as of yet, asked her anything about her life; they'd clearly dismissed her as ornamental. For the first half-hour after they'd arrived, she'd watched the others talk while a part of her observed Steve and Gloria's strange living room. It reminded her of her grade-two time capsule project in which a small office safe, not unlike those sold at Staples, was filled with newspapers, canned goods, a Walkman, a Nirvana cassette and a flannel grunge shirt.

Steve and Gloria's living room seemed to have been sealed somewhere between Richard Burton and Elizabeth Taylor's first and second divorce. Magazines on the coffee table touted new fiction by John Cheever. The Plexiglas cover of the turntable in the corner had become fully opaque from dust, while the spines of nearby vinyl records were illegible from solar bleaching. Brittany had also noticed the total absence of any sort of personal imagery—family photos, portraits, drawings. And if she squinted, she could see a slight nicotine glaze coating all surfaces in the room. She had absentmindedly picked up a small figurine from a side table, and it made a small clicking sound as she removed it, severing its decade-long bonds of wax buildup, dust and stasis.

Since the megasuccess of Kyle's novel the year before, Brittany had become accustomed to her new invisibility. During the years Kyle had laboured in obscurity, Brittany had supported him—and had been sure of her place in the world. Now he was famous, and their lives had become filled with expensive trips and meals and visits with the rich, witty and renowned, all of which was beginning to bore her.

Then Steve had surprised Brittany. Just when she was feeling her most invisible, her favourite writer in the world took almost an hour to provide her with copious, thrilling background information on each of his five novels. She felt drunk with privilege as he spoke and spoke and spoke. It was almost as if he was speaking only to her, ignoring Kyle and Gloria completely. Kyle could never understand Brittany's love of Steve's work—nor, for that matter, could Brittany—but love and admiration can't always be explained.

When Steve had finished, Brittany was dazed and happy. She was mostly content to listen when Steve and Kyle went on to have a manly discussion of literature. When Steve went into the kitchen to see about dinner, Brittany followed him, noting in passing that there seemed to be no evidence of food in the offing. Steve was poking about inside a cupboard.

"Steve," said Brittany, "do you ever read works in progress?"

Steve looked surprised. "Sometimes."

"Kyle has a working draft of his new novel with him. Would you give it a peek? I'm sure he'd love to hear your opinion. It's in his satchel, over with our coats."

"Brittany, Kyle is such a young writer, and the opinion of an éminence grise such as myself might skew his growth and distinctiveness."

"I can't help but feel he'd benefit from your reading, Steve."

"It's better I don't get involved."

"You are so sensitive, Steve."

"Now you go join the others while I get dinner cracking."

"Thanks, Steve."

Glove Pond: Steve

Steve's fevered brain was contemplating how to make dinner out of beweeviled pancake mix when young Brittany gave him an excuse to procrastinate. The moment she left the kitchen, he raced to the coat closet and ferreted out the copy of unsavoury Falconcrest's upcoming book from its satchel. *Curse him and his new ideas.*

Locked within the warm, breezeless confines of the guest bathroom, Steve began to read:

Love in the Age of Office Superstores
Chapter One

Shimmering amber millipedes of dawn light chewed on the office superstore's blank stucco outer walls. A lone pigeon fell to the parking lot, scavenged for edible grit, found none, then returned to the roof and out of sight, possibly to die of boredom. Formless overcast clouds the colour of Korean paper-shredding machines inched in from the west. In the spotless front seat of his Chevy Lumina sedan sat Norm. He was no longer young, his pot-belly enblubbered roughly to the extent of a large Thanksgiving turkey. His scalp grew hair like virulent beige bread mould. His hands clasped a Diet Coke filled with house-brand vodka—breakfast and lunch folded together into one meal.

The car radio played "Wake Me Up Before You Go Go!," a tune from Norm's youth that, in some indefinable way, reminded him that he was a captive of his life's bleak repeat cycle. Other cars pulled into the lot, fellow morning shifters, their vehicles neither new nor spotless: Jettas made from sheets of rusty lace, polio-stricken Corollas from the early 1990s, and late 1980s Chryslers held together by local AM radio station promotional stickers and wishful thinking. Yes, Norm's colleagues had youth, but Norm's maroon Lumina had the capacity to drive across a dozen ecosystems on a single tank of gas without the slightest threat of breakdown. When nuclear war finally arrived and everyone else's shit heap died trying to escape the firestorm, it was in Norm's car that everyone would ride, stylishly and comfortably.

The vodka tasted harsh, scientific and aggressively cheap. Technically, vodka was made from potatoes, yet Norm suspected his was made by underpaid robots on some distant sci-fi planet where living organisms had long ago ceased to exist, and where the recipe for vodka was the legacy of long-vanished humanoid Elders. Potato-like molecules may have entered the vodka-making process, but the possibility of genuine tuber content was nil. But despite his vodka's best-left-unimagined lineage, Norm required it to survive the day ahead.

A trailer full of Dell products sat in the superstore's loading dock, ready to suckle the building with its abundance. Norm dreaded Dell Day almost as much—but not quite as much—as he dreaded Office Furniture Shipment Day with its lumbar-destroying monotony of unloading, carton-breaking and inventorying the shipment's contents. Should Norm ever have need of an office—a dream that felt as unattainable as spending a month's holiday with Smurfs—it would certainly not be furnished with an L-shaped plastic/walnut laminated Chinese fibreboard modular desk system graced by a Dell. No, Norm's dream office would contain a simple pine table, a humble bottle of ink and a quill made from a griffin's wing feather.

One final sip and Norm knew it was time to leave his Lumina. Leaving his Lumina was harder for Norm than getting out of bed in the morning. Preparing to leave his Lumina reminded him of the gestation of a dragon's egg, which sat soft and inert for twenty months, only hardening during the final days before hatching. After one goodbye vodka swig, Norm opened the driver's door a crack and paused as the November air bled into the vehicle and he exchanged the tinny sounds of early 1980s pop music supersensation, Wham!, for cold and discomfort.

Moments later, clad in his scarlet employee's shirt, a shivering Norm plopped out of the Chevy and limped and hobbled and shuffled and dragged his carcass towards the superstore. Its automated door whisked open with a dry hiss reminiscent of soil being tossed onto a coffin. Instantly, the change in light quality informed his reptile cortex that he was no longer in the natural world. Human faces became cruel Toby jugs of ignorance and buffoonery, with nostril hairs that dangled small, hard rosin nuggets. The uncirculated air prepared to garner its daily load of invisible fart galaxies, which perpetually placed nearby shoppers beneath cloaks of suspicion. Post-it Notes sat in their bins, daydreaming about daydreams. At the ends of aisles 1 and 2, crisp totems built of reams of bond paper dreamed of one day bearing sonnets and the solutions to string theory, yet in their hearts—if reams of paper can be said to possess hearts—they knew they would, at best, merely tout a daily seafood special or be the unread, unloved third page of an in-house corporate document on earthquake preparedness—and even fates such as these were probably too much to expect. Instead, they would end up as a discarded second draft of a homework assignment on manganese or pollination, badly formatted and crumpled up, tossed into a wastepaper basket alongside lumps of chewed gum, pubic hair trimmings, Kotex wrappers and the lids of cranapple juice bottles.

Norm stood by the gum racks and the numerous impulse point-of-purchase displays near the front tills. He idly fondled a chocolate stain embedded in his crimson shirt, unwashed from the day before. He cocked an ear, trying to identify the PA system's first musical gem of the day ("Every Little Thing She Does Is Magic," by the Police), heard the clatter of a pile of CD and DVD jewel cases falling onto the white tile floors at the store's farthest end, heard the rumble of shopping carts being corralled into their marshalling stalls. He turned around, his midriff jiggling like a Jell-O mould, and tried to decide which brand of gum he was going to steal that morning.

DeeDee

I don't think you're a monster, Roger, and I am not a monster either. I am, in fact, one of those mothers who clips inspiring articles from newspapers, hoards them, and then pounces on her offspring with a stack of twenty—usually when they're in a hurry and their heads are in the completely wrong space to appreciate them. There's that old *Kids in the Hall* skit where the overprotective mother goes through a new copy of *TV Guide* to highlight with a yellow marker all of the shows she thinks her son will like. That's me. Or rather, that's me these days. I wasn't always such a good mother.

Bethany told me about something you wrote, about how animals are the voices of the dead come to speak to us. I don't know if they're here to console us or to warn us and scare the crap out of us. I like animals. They're better than people. Even when they're mean they're pure, whereas people, when they're mean, are simply lost.

Did you know that Bethany's stepbrother hanged himself? Oh, that was awful. Devon. He was a lost soul. Bethany found his body. He did it with the twenty-five-foot orange extension cord from the leaf blower, strung on the chandelier in the front hallway. She looked at him for a half-hour before she phoned anybody.

Chandelier: that sounds so swanky, but it wasn't. That was when I was married to Kenny and we were living in this *Brady Bunch* house in an okay suburb. I woke up every morning with my stomach clenching. Why? Because I felt like a useless member of society and I could feel the ghosts of the people who built the *Brady Bunch* suburb surrounding me. I knew they were better people than I'd ever be: industrious, optimistic and dutiful—and I could feel them judging me. I could never live up to the expectations of people who built such cheerful, well-laid-out 3BDRs with dormer windows, rhododendrons and garages lined with pegboard where the tools could be alphabetically arranged, and where orange extension cords always had a special cord-only spot above the pesticide cupboard. I couldn't enter the garage because of that goddam pegboard wall, and because I was spooked I'd meet the ghost of the guy who installed it. The ghost would see me, and he'd know that Kenny beat me with full plastic bottles of fabric softener, that Kenny hectored and teased his son, who hanged himself because of it, and that Kenny treated Bethany as if she didn't exist—literally, like that game you play with kids where you pretend you're unable to see them, except that Kenny did this all the time. I think this is why Bethany wears all that Goth makeup and pretends not to care—it's a testament to my lack of care back then.

God, *Kenny*—he feels like forever ago. Not even a ghost. Listen to me: ghosts, ghosts and ghosts. I often wonder if I'm genuinely haunted.

Bethany's first friend, Becky, died of cancer. I remember that, but if I'm honest, I was more wrapped up in taking Bethany's father to the cleaners after he left us. I can't even put a face on Becky, though she was doubtless cute as a button.

I got zippo in the divorce because Reid (that was his name) was ~~a shitty businessman~~ broke—oh, there was some furniture, and the minivan was paid for, but that was it.

A year later, both of Bethany's grandfathers died within five days of each other. What are the chances of that? My father hit an oncoming semi-trailer loaded with raw telephone poles on the 99. Grandpa Mike, Reid's father, had a kidney stone so big and sharp it sliced his kidney from within. The slice got infected with some drug-resistant bug, and within thirty-six hours it was curtains. Ever done two funerals in one week? Not fun. Especially if you're not wanted at one of them, and especially if all the family members involved with the other funeral are unstabilized psychos off their meds.

About a year after the funerals I married Catastrophe Number Two, Eamon, a handsome devil, but a devil. His daughter was a sweet thing named Julie, and her nineteenth birthday was the same day as our wedding, I remember that. A few months later her life partner, Jed, clobbered her and then threw her out a window. Her shinbone punctured her lung. He's eligible for parole in 2028.

That Thanksgiving my mother died of emphysema. We knew Mom's death was coming. Bethany, I might add, pretty much lived in the hospital for a month, taking care of Mom. She is a good kid. I don't deserve her. That is my mantra: *I don't deserve her.*

If I remember correctly, next Mr. Van Buren, Bethany's band teacher, got killed—another car crash on the 99, driving up to Whistler. They should throw that highway into the trash and build a new one. It's cursed.

Oh, hell, then Kurt Cobain blew out his brains, and then Ginger and Snowbelle—our pair of twin Persians— got diabetes and we couldn't afford the treatment and that was that. Bethany was sixteen or so when two of her pals smoked dope laced with angel dust. Cops found their bodies in the duck lagoon at Ambleside.

By then I'd divorced Eamon and married Kenny, and a year after that is when Devon hanged himself from the chandelier with an electrical cord.

Shit.

I'm going to pour myself a drink.

My sister, Paulette, was next, and she is, I promise, the last death I'm going to tell you about. I hated that woman, but boy, I loved her too. Her primary means of expressing emotion was sponging stencilled Mother Gooses onto the dado of your guest bedroom. Or showing up at barbecues with potpourri gift baskets shaped like frogs wearing Ray-Bans. She had no sense of humour, **none!!!**

But then at the dinner table one night (Paulette cooked, even when she came over to my house), Kenny made a joke about Muppets in a leather bar and Paulette laughed, and the two of them hit it off, and I was so jealous I thought my eyeballs would pop like popcorn. Paulette had married some wimpy dude named Miles back when she was twenty-two, divorced after three months and never remarried. I think she was a dyke, but what's done is done.

Even after Kenny and I divorced, he remained the best of pals with Paulette. I bumped into them once, coming out of a Meg Ryan movie at the Esplanade Six theatre. Almost in stereo, they said, "I don't buy that Meg/perkiness thing any more," and off they went, riffing away while I shot invisible Drano-tipped pitchforks at their backs from my forehead.

During Paulette's breast cancer, I was a wreck, but so was Kenny. It was almost like a sitcom, the way the two of us tried to "out-care" each other on Paulette's behalf, while at the same time avoiding each other. We were both seeking out the usual stuff: vitamin therapies, inspirational paperbacks, online breaking news on experimental treatments, wacky get-well cards and lymph masseuses—all of this while Bethany did the meat and mashed potatoes stuff like picking things up and delivering Paulette to the chemo sessions. Yet again, I was drunk with self-centredness and Bethany paid the price.

In the end, we did the usual nothing-ventured-nothing-gained stuff: Mexico, herbalists in Manitoba, a child in South Carolina who would breathe a miracle onto your loved one's photo for a twenty-dollar donation. But the cancer was one of those forest-fire varieties.

Roger, I am not a monster, but I *am* tired and I am now officially drunk.

If Bethany helps you in writing your novel, then that's a wonderful thing. But if you hurt her in any way, I will kill you.

DeeDee
(DD)

Glove Pond: Gloria

Brittany followed Steve into the kitchen, leaving Kyle Falconcrest to sit on the sofa beside Gloria, who seized this opportunity to bombard the young author with question after question after question about his writing habits, his characters, his personal life and his opinions about her opinions. He was obviously riveted, and he chose to sit mostly silent, letting Gloria do the driving. All too soon, Brittany came back into the room, putting an end to their glorious engagement.

"How's dinner coming?" Gloria asked.

"It was hard to tell," Brittany said. "I'm not much of a cook. I work, so Kyle and I mostly eat deli food. Or order in—when we're not out at parties and galas and dinners." She sighed.

Young Brittany looked unhappy. "Brittany, you appear troubled—"

"It's nothing."

"No," said Gloria. "Nothing is always something." She felt like Noël Coward for having uttered such a witticism—or Edward Albee, or the Bard. She stared up at her book collection. *I love calling Shakespeare "the Bard." It makes me feel like I have a personal relationship with him, one that's far superior to other peoples'*—

~~personal relationships with him~~. She looked at *The Complete Works of William Shakespeare*, a 259-volume set bound in unborn pigskin. *I remember the day I bought those—Steve and I on our honeymoon in the swan-filled, ambiance-rich town of Stratford-upon-Avon in England. Everywhere I looked—culture! Culture! Culture! And one of these days, pending a break in my busy acting schedule, I'm going to read one of those books.*

Oh, right. She'd been asking if Brittany was feeling troubled about something.

"I think it's stress," the young woman confessed.

"I thought you seemed blue," said Gloria, noticing that Kyle took this chance to pour himself a Scotch and excuse himself to look more closely at the bookcases.

"Come on, Brittany, tell me everything."

"It's just that . . . I've been performing so many surgeries lately, and with Kyle's schedule, too, it's just so hard to keep on top of things."

"Surgery? A woman performing surgery?"

"Yes, I'm a surgeon."

"Really! I'd never have guessed—a surgeon—we gals sure are coming a long way these days. Are you a specialist?"

"I mostly do brain surgery—elective brain surgery. But I'm starting to move into oncological surgery—the removal of cancerous growths."

"I think I have a remedy for your stress."

"A remedy? Really?"

"Yes. Come with me."

Gloria motioned for Brittany to come with her up the stairs. Kyle looked up, but Gloria waved him off.

"No, no, young man, gals only. You stay down here and have noble ideas and enjoy our large and diverse book collection."

"Right. Will do." Kyle gulped a finger-and-a-half of Scotch while Gloria led Brittany up the stairs and into her boudoir. The smothering sensation of scents and dry powder on her face and in her nose made Brittany cough.

"You poor thing," said Gloria. "Have a seat."

Gloria pulled up a guest tuffet beside her chair, a chunky silk bonbon. "Let's put some makeup on you right now, young lady. Makeup is the answer to your problems."

"Makeup? I never wear makeup."

"Well, from now on you will. Your unmodified eyes remind me of newly born pink mice, and, my dear, I think you have approximately one-third of a pimple near the corner of your nose."

"That's Helen."

"You name your pimples?"

"This one I do. Helen is this pimple that migrates around my face but never quite leaves."

"My dear, Helen must die."

"I don't understand makeup, Gloria—why wear it at all? Isn't it dishonest?"

"My dear, the reason we wear makeup is to prevent the world from seeing what we're like underneath."

"What's wrong with that?"

"What's wrong with *that*?" Gloria was in the midst of swishing about a small sand dune of face powder in a cerise lacquered box. "My dear, if you allow your feelings to be exposed, people will hurt you with them.

They will use your feelings against you. Something once private and sacred to you will be transformed into a weapon. Something precious will be damaged. You will experience pain."

Brittany looked sombre.

"Now, may I put some powder on your forehead?" Gloria asked.

"Yes."

Roger

Not the best day.

This morning I had one of those from-hell wake-ups where all you can think of is fear and loss and the people you've hurt and all the damage you've done. You put your hand out from under the sheets and the air is cold. It's like not wanting to be born. And then, finally, your head can't stand lying there thinking any more, so you jump up and run to the bathroom and put your head under the shower's jet, hoping it will fuzz out the feelings, but instead there's only a tiny amount of diversion.

I get older. I grow old. Somebody starts to tell me about their dreams, and I get so bored I have to escape. I flee to the craft superstore down the street from the hardware superstore, down the parkway from the office superstore. I wander its aisles, looking for the seed of an idea to help me escape from myself—I walk past artificial lilies and unpainted birdhouses and crewel kits that allow me to make images of koi swimming in Tokyo ponds. And then, in the scrapbooking aisle, I see 79¢ sticker packs with little rainbows and unicorns that say DREAMS CAN COME TRUE! and it makes me want to cry the way we feed nonsense crap like this to kids, who are going to inherit a century of ugly wars started by people who died long ago, but who were sick and damaged enough to transmit their hatred down through the centuries. Dreams don't come true. Dreams die. Dreams get compromised. Dreams end up dealing meth in a booth at the back of the Olive Garden. Dreams choke to death on bay leaves. Dreams get spleen cancer.

So there you have it—that's been my day until now. The Dell shipment got stuck at customs and won't be arriving until tomorrow, so I'm going to have a vodka snack and pretend to help customers in the office furniture department. Then I'll probably go through the aisles and look at all the plastic crap we sell and wonder about the chemicals in it, and what leftovers were flushed into the water system during manufacturing. I sometimes get the feeling that we're having full-time one-on-one unprotected sex with the twenty-first century, exchanging fluids with the era: antibiotics, swimming pool chlorine, long-chain molecules, gas fumes, new car smell—all of it one great big condom-free involuntary love-in.

Roger

A half-hour later: Pete is away this afternoon, so we're all slacking off like crazy. We drew straws to see who works the till, and Kyle lost. I went down the road and bought a bottle of rotgut vodka and am going to work on *Glove Pond* in the loading bay. It's warm as long as you're not in the wind.

R.

Glove Pond: Kyle

Steve and Gloria were psychic abortions. Steve's hour-long exegesis of his five grotesque, directionless and archaic novels reminded Kyle of his sulpha allergy—of that day at his sister's wedding barbecue when he took a tablet for his infected hangnail and suddenly felt as if he were itching and burning to death from the inside. Jumping in the pool only fed the fire. He remembered screaming for painkillers in the ambulance before he blacked out. He more or less blacked out during Steve's speech, only to wake up and find Gloria sitting beside him, her leftmost talon rubbing his right inner thigh. She informed him that he wasn't as in command of his father figure metaphors as he thought—but that was okay because Gloria had figured out how he could hone his skills on this matter in the future.

Thank the Lord Brittany rescued him and a further encroachment of the talons, and thank the Lord she'd then gone upstairs. All the tea in China wouldn't make him go up and have a look at what that car crash of a souse was up to.

His stomach gurgled. How come there was no odour of cooking? Nor evidence of catering? Nor even place settings at the dusty dining table? Kyle went to the kitchen to investigate. No Steve. All he could find was an empty box of Triscuits on the counter and a cookie sheet in the sink. An empty plastic Safeway cheddar cheese wrapper with little gouges in it lay on the floor, as though abandoned by teeny white-trash mice. The stove elements were cold. He looked in the fridge. *How is possible to have nothing in a fridge except a jar of pickle juice?*

He wondered what the dinner strategy was, and then he realized that there *was* no dinner strategy. All these people had in the house was Scotch. This realization was shocking to Kyle, and he sat down at the kitchen table to collect his thoughts.

A furnace kicked in with a faint hum. He heard a car pass on the road out front. The fridge burped into low gear, and Kyle had a depressing vision of penguins protecting stillborn eggs. This was possibly the creepiest room he had ever been in.

What about the cupboards—could they be as empty as the fridge? *No. That's simply not possible. There has to be food—some kind of food—somewhere in the kitchen.*

He went to the cupboards, and each one was revealed to be empty until behind the fifth door he saw a box— Willamette's Homestyle Pancake Batter Mix. On its front was the most shockingly inappropriate image of— there were no other words to describe it—a plantation darkie offering a platter of flapjacks to a lace-clad Nicole Kidman of yore, who hid behind both a pink fan and the easy knowledge that she could have her darkie flayed to death at whim. The box had no bar code. Kyle opened its flaps and saw what looked like tiny dancing flakes of oregano.

Oh dear God!

He dropped the box on the counter, and weevils scattered away from it in all directions.

Steve walked into the room. "Oh, so you're a chef then—what good luck for us."

Bethany

Kyle told me that he thinks Staples is a piece of shit and should burn. I'm shocked to find that Trail Mix Boy has an anarchist spark in him. Granted, he was baked on mushrooms when he said it, and he and I and eight others were ready to mutiny after a twenty-minute seminar on toner cartridge recycling. When I look back on my childhood and on the pictures I once had in my head about what adult life would be like, they weren't of Fahad squinting into a coffee spoon to see if his blackheads were visible while a Ricoh sales rep demonstrated by way of a PowerPoint presentation that cartridges take a thousand years to decompose in a landfill.

Okay, then, Bethany, what were *your images?*

Thank you, interior monologue. I thought that when I was an adult I'd somehow be a bit more connected to life and death—that when I went to bed at night, after drinking a cup of chilled blood with my husband, Johnny Depp, I would look back on a day filled with confessions and accidents and affairs and large amounts of money travelling in all directions. Instead, I get to watch the assistant manager's QuickTime loop of Blair being caught stealing Chiclets on the securi-cam. The soundtrack? "We Are Family" by Sister Sledge. At least in a possible future career as a nurse, the daily drudgery might be balanced by the possibility of genuine human drama.

But here at Shtooples, there's no chance of drama, period.

Thank you again, interior monologue. You are correct.

So, then, what's keeping you here?

Inertia. Laziness. Hormones. Habit.

Habit? I thought you said you wanted drama.

Yeah, well, aren't we human beings screwy creatures? At least at Shtooples the worst thing that can happen to you is that you get fired. Nobody dies at Shtooples. Nothing can ever truly fuck up in Aisle 5-South. It's safe. In its way.

Are you finally sick of death?

Please, don't ask me.

But I have to, and I won't stop asking until you answer me.

Okay, yeah, I am sick of it. Happy now?

Happy is a hokey concept at best, Bethany.

Okay, then, are you satisfied?

The truth is always satisfying.

Why is that?

I don't know. It's the way the universe is built.

Wouldn't it be great if we all lived in a world where everybody believed everyone else's lies? The lies would cancel each other out, and you'd be left with a massive ultratruth.

Snorrrrrrre. Are you baked on mushrooms too, Bethany?

No. I'm wondering how much longer I can handle working here at das Shtoop.

Nursing school?

I don't know. Anything. Unemployment? Unwed pregnancy?

You're too classy to take the easy ways out, Bethany.

Okay, interior monologue, if you're so smart, provide me with a suggestion.

What's wrong with school?

No response

. . . Bethany? . . . School?

I'm thinking.

Well, technically, I'm the one who's thinking here.

I don't have any money, and I don't want my mother to sell her place merely to rescue me from prison.

Now we're getting somewhere.

Gee, thanks.

What would be so wrong with your mother selling her condo? The market's good right now. She could rent a place.

Let's stop right now.

Bethany?

Look, there's Fahad, and he's trying out a new pore-cleansing strip by the sink. Gotta go.

PS: Roger, my mother wrote you yet another letter?

PPS: I think about *Glove Pond* all the time. I'm trying to figure out who is who. Am I Brittany? Is Kyle Kyle? Are you Steve? Or maybe I'm partially Kyle or . . . you're so lucky to have an imagination, Roger. You can sit down and make shit up. I can't even make up my mind.

PPPS: As part of my efforts to help Kyle cope with death, we went to visit his grandmother's grave. We were reading tombstones together, and I said it must be nice to be dead and not have to worry about how you look any more—as a joke. And Kyle said to me, "I saw this show on the Discovery Channel, and it said that beauty isn't only about the traits you possess, it's also about the traits you don't possess." He then said, "You're really beautiful, Bethany, because there are so many bad traits a lot of girls have and you don't have any of them."

I asked him, "Like what?"

"You're not greedy. And you don't plot or scheme, and you don't go all slutty or manipulative if you don't get what you want."

I didn't know what to say, so I didn't say anything, but I've been floating ever since.

DeeDee

To: Roger Thorpe
c/o: Staples

Roger,
Me again. This morning I had a crown replaced ($$$!), and throughout the experience I read your *Glove Pond*. Bethany gave me a photocopy of your manuscript. I must admit, Roger, it's too highbrow for me—all the talk about literature—out of my league. How do you have

the patience to write? Me—I'm not calm enough to read fiction. I think you have to be in the right state of mind, and I haven't been there since I was fourteen. I can read magazines and newspapers and other factual stuff. I'm actually leaving library books about science all over the house. It's an obvious ploy to get Bethany interested in school, but it does work, especially the books I leave near the toilet. They always get thumbed through, and it gives us things to talk about besides reality TV and the past. There's this one book on the stars that's fascinating, and it got me onto Google, looking up all sorts of things. Do you have any idea how big the universe is, Roger? It's terrifying, and the only thing I can think of that might make it not terrifying is the possibility of life all over the place. I mean, if life was an accident on this one little planet in the middle of nowhere, then what's the point? I find it hard to believe that human beings are the crowning achievement of life on earth. Something better than us has to come along. Maybe someday there'll be a flower the size of Colorado—or a marine organism that occupies the entire Indian Ocean— massive supercreatures that use telepathy to speak with other creatures in other galaxies!

Here's my final thought: how come there are only a tiny number of planets orbiting the sun? If you were to take all the planets and squish them into a ball, it'd still only be one-billionth the size of the sun. Brother, I mean, why not have no planets at all? If you're going to have planets, have a thousand of them for every star!

DD

PS: Can you stress the importance of education with Bethany? I'll sell the condo in a flash to pay for it, so don't let her plead poverty.

Thank you, Roger.

"You weren't going to serve us dinner."

"That's not true."

"Do you have a surprise platter of cold cuts and Danish cheese concealed in the den? Or do I hear a rotisserie broiling Cornish game hens in the garage?"

"No need to be snarky about it."

"So you admit it!"

"We were going to feed you dinner."

"And that dinner would have been what . . . *pancakes*?"

Some of the more brazen weevils were scampering across the counter and reboarding the mothership. "I was going to make crepes."

"You *what?*"

"Thin, perfectly shaped crepes—elegant yet substantial—filled with a marmalade reduction."

"You liar. You don't have any marmalade. I checked out your fridge. It might as well be abandoned in a vacant lot."

"I was going to borrow marmalade from our next-door neighbour. Last spring they borrowed all of our jams and jellies for a toast party, and they owe us. How was I to know the pancake mix was a haven for vermin?

Now my plans are dashed. Perhaps you could spot me a hundred dollars for Chinese food."

"You're nuts."

Like an elderly man dying in his sleep, the furnace suddenly stopped. The fridge stopped humming. No cars drove by the house. Kyle stared at Steve.

Steve said, "Think of Brittany and Gloria. They deserve something better than tap water for dinner, don't you think? Please, look into your heart and think of them."

Kyle considered this. "You manipulative old soak. Okay, whatever. This is a college town—they always have good takeout. Do you have a Yellow Pages?"

Steve walked to a side table, picked up the phone book and handed it to Kyle.

"Chinese or pizza?" asked Kyle.

"Chinese," said Steve. "You get more leftovers and they last longer."

"Fine."

Kyle ordered Chinese food and then joined Steve in the living room.

Steve stood at the bottom of the staircase, looking up. "Here come our ladies."

Kyle looked up. "Brittany?"

Brittany had been radically transformed through cosmetics and wardrobe. What had once been a prim, orderly face was now a voluptuous Hollywood mask, with carmine Cupid's bow lips, turquoise eyeshadow à la Cleopatra, thick, juicy false eyelashes and skin as pale and flawless as a ~~pre–global warming Vermont ski slope~~ winter mountain slope. Gloria had loaned her a platinum blonde wig of near drag-queen grandeur; ~~one that~~

~~might suitably have been worn to the launch of a *Queen Mary* voyage circa 1961.~~ Her little black dress had been replaced with a strapless rouched ivory-coloured silk body-hugger—Marilyn Monroe being photographed for *Life* magazine. Within the gentle glow of a room lit mostly by unreplaced dead light bulbs, Brittany now crackled with movie star energy.

"Hello, Kyle."

"Whoa."

"Hello, Steve," Brittany said. "Are we eating soon?"

Gloria was behind Brittany. "Now *this* is a woman. Forget today's trampy little sluts walking around in dental floss and fabric scraps—a *real* woman has verve. A *real* woman leaves chaos in her wake."

Kyle said, "Brittany . . . what are you *doing*?"

Steve interrupted: "Take *that*, Julie Christie! Take *that* Charlotte Rampling!" ~~Take *that*, Natalie Wood! Take *that*, Sophia Loren! [Verna Lisi? Angie Dickinson?]~~

Kyle turned to Steve. "Who on *earth* are you talking about?" He turned back to Brittany. "Brit, you look like a gold digger from a Cary Grant movie." He cupped his right hand to his ear: "Hey, I think there's a rich plutocrat in the kitchen who'll give you a fifty to visit the powder room."

"Thank you for supporting my new look, Kyle. And screw you. This is fun."

Steve wolf-whistled.

"Thank you, Steve." Brittany walked into the living room as Gloria plucked invisible dander from Brittany's shoulder. She sat on the sofa. "I needed a change—and I need a Scotch. Steve?"

"Coming right up."

Gloria asked for a Scotch as well. Kyle said, "Jesus, do you people *douche* with Scotch? I can't believe you."

"Kyle, be quiet. We're talking about me, not you. And speaking of me, I'm *sick* of being me. I'm sick of my job and I'm sick of my point of view and I'm sick of the interior voice in my head that never really changes from one year to the next."

"You hear voices?" Gloria asked.

"You know what I mean, Gloria—we all have it—that little voice that debates which bridge to take to get to work in the morning, the voice that narrates a book in your head when you're reading. And I'm just so sick of it! So tonight I'm Elizabeth Taylor."

"You look ravishing," said Gloria.

"Here's a Scotch."

"Thank you, Steve."

"Scotch, Kyle?"

"*Brother.*"

Kyle looked annoyed and Steve said, "Why so snippy? And besides, alcohol seems to be a big theme in your work. On page one of your new book, the main character's already hitting the bottle."

"What the hell—you read part of my new book? Is that where you were?"

Brittany looked at Steve. "Steve—did you plunder Kyle's manuscript from his satchel and read part of it?"

Steve was caught.

Kyle shouted, "I can't believe this—you stole a copy of my first chapter?"

"Don't be testy," said Steve. "We're both writers. Is

it wrong to want to share tips on craftsmanship with a peer?"

"How did you even know I had it with me?"

"I told him, Kyle."

"Why'd you do that?"

"How could it hurt? And you could use the advice of someone other than me."

"I like your advice."

"Have you ever wondered, Kyle, what sort of burden your need for feedback puts on me? I have almost no free time, and when I do get some it's all totally sucked into your bottomless well of writer's neediness." She looked at her two hosts. "I tell you, there are chapters lying around the house like autumn leaves. Everywhere. Always. On the couch. On the stove. On the toilet. In the car. On the StairMaster. In the breakfast nook. On the floor—*especially* on the floor. You'd think we decorated our house with an electric fan and a Staples gift certificate." She turned to Gloria. "And all of these chapters are shingled with Post-it Notes, all of them highlighted in yellows and pinks and blues, and every little Post-it Note is asking me what I think or what I suggest."

Gloria thought, *What's a Post-It Note?*

"Fine," said Kyle.

There was a pause. They could all hear each other sipping their drinks as they watched passing car headlights zoom up the living-room walls, only to vanish on the ceiling. Kyle broke the silence. "So—Steve—seeing as you read it and all, what did you think?"

"I think there's Chinese food coming soon," said Steve.

"Good," said Gloria, making no effort to fetch plates or cutlery.

"What about the book?" Kyle asked. "I *know* you've read part of it."

Steve paused. What *did* he think of Kyle's book? All of the pop culture references had been totally lost on him, and with all of the technology it discussed, Steve had felt like he'd been reading a NASA manual on how to fix a lunar rover. However, "I do think you tapped into something universal," he said. "The not wanting to get out of bed aspect of the first chapter. The notion of no longer wanting to go on with life and wondering what possible benefit could come of decades and decades of life past one's prime when all of life's big strokes have been made, when one is left only with regrets and no options. *That* I liked—the sensation that grief is like a werewolf that moves into your house one day and never leaves, and every time you open a door or round a corner, it's there, lying in wait."

"Really?" said Kyle.

"Yes," said Steve.

"Huh."

"You see," said Brittany, "it's not so bad getting another opinion."

"You're right," said Kyle.

Everyone sipped, and then Brittany changed the subject. "In the closet I saw a football," she said. "Do you two have children?"

Although technically nothing was happening, the room came to a stop. Steve and Gloria darted eyes at each other. Gloria said, "Um, yes. We have a lovely child."

"Yes," said Steve. "A lovely, lovely child. Just one."

"How interesting," said Kyle. "Boy or girl?"

Steve and Gloria made eye contact before Steve answered, "A boy."

"He's never mentioned on your book jacket flaps," said Brittany.

The doorbell rang.

"Dinner's here," said Steve.

Bethany

Roger,

Unlike Brittany, I don't mind test-reading your book at all! In fact, *Glove Pond* is now officially a part of my life, and I'd like to share it with other people, but who . . . Kyle? He'll never be the reading type. My other fellow Shtooples inmates? No way—this is too special. So that leaves my mom.

I wish I had something *I'd* made that I wanted to keep special for myself, Roger. You're lucky—you have the book. My only writing class ever was a disaster. I chucked out almost everything the afternoon I returned home from the last one. Sheer disgust. Golden lining: at least my couple of years of toil at the community college allows me course credits if I go back to study nursing as a "mature student." Yes, I'm still thinking about it.

The one thing I did keep from my writing class was my essay on toast being buttered—"from the toast's point of view." I include it here in this envelope. Think of it as a fellow writer's inspiration to another fellow writer. Wait—that last sentence came out wrong.

As they say in cheesy restaurants everywhere, Roger, "Enjoy!"

Bethany

Toast

I deserve better than to be forced to document my cruel fate at the hands of a pat of butter. What crime did I ever commit, except being crispy and golden brown on the outside—bearing the faintest bouquet of carbon—while being tender, fluffy and white, nay, cloudlike, on the inside?

And like I can't see the knife coming my way! If you wanted to scare me, it worked, and . . . oh jeez . . . it's not even butter, it's margarine. Oh dear God, it's not even margarine—it's a *spread*—house-brand spread, bought from a Costco, at that. That's all I get in the end? Butter-like spread-type bulk-purchased yellow goop? I don't even rate butter? Thanks. Thanks a *lot*. At least butter is a classy way to go. Even margarine has a certain Volvo cachet.

Well, that's life. During my childhood as a humble slice inside the loaf (four slices in from the front), I once had dreams. Maybe one day, as toast, I would bear an image of Jesus or, if not Jesus, then NASCAR racing legend Dale Earnhardt or, failing that, Catherine Zeta-Jones. Instead, all I display is a golden brown toastiness distributed across my heated surface with about the same degree of randomness as craters on the moon, with a slightly darker browning in my midriff where I bowed slightly towards the toaster's equatorial grill.

I think it's actually mean to trick young bread slices into thinking that they, too, might one day harbour toast faces, let alone be sold on eBay for thousands of dollars and make a wacky news story that goes viral.

Life generally blows. I mean, don't get me wrong, there are far worse ways to go than as toast—croutons and stuffing spring to mind—as well as the worst fate of all: blue mould, followed by a few hasty twists of the bread bag's neck, then you're plunged into the trash and live in an anaerobic limbo until the year AD 327,406, when a glacier scours you out of what was once the local landfill. My fate is to be toast. I suppose that's a small blessing.

Wait—wait—it's almost here, the knife. It's almost ready to dock onto my super-sensitive spot in the dead centre of my—nmghhh . . . aughGHHH!

Oh!

That was—

That was—

Do it again.

Oh *God*, they never told us about this, back in the loaf. Jesus, I'm crumbling all over the place.

I don't care.

Mnmmmglmph!

Ahhhhh . . .

Warm, drizzling rivulets soak my being; molten, swirling, sun-coloured puddles drench my cracked, scabby and burnt skin—my death so near. Already I can sense teeth coming my way, and yet the fear is gone. I feel free! I feel dirty! I feel submissive! I feel . . .

I feel . . .

I feel . . .

. . . the end.

C+

Bethany, I didn't totally <u>feel</u> like I was being buttered, like I really <u>was</u> the toast. As a writer, you have to <u>empathize</u>. At Thursday's workshop, I want you to listen to some of the other butterings that will be read aloud. They'll give you a better feel on how to connect with your protagonist. I think that, collectively, we will arrive at a satisfying creative solution.

Bethany

Roger,
You've missed five days at work now. Why are you skipping work so much? Are you sick? I feel ridiculous leaving correspondence in your basement suite's mail slot, but I've got no intention of knocking on your door. Leaving you this note is the extent of my act of reaching out to you.

My theory is that you're not sick at all. I think you're sitting inside your place, getting hosed and cursing the universe, probably because you're mad at your ex-wife and her lawyer.

I think you're going through a bad patch, but I also think you'll be out of it soon, so I'm going to write this and stick it through your door and then not worry about you any more. You're certainly not missing anything at work, but I did this one freaky thing you might find interesting—and of possible use to you as a novelist.

After going to visit Kyle's grandmother's grave, I got to thinking about death more than usual, and I figure that someday you'll write the words THE END and *Glove Pond* will be finished. That's got to be sort of like death, don't you think? And unlike real life, in a book, you know exactly when the end is going to happen.

And because you know when the end is coming, you'll maybe feel some sort of pressure near the end, like, *Holy shit! This puppy's going to be finished in maybe five pages! No three pages! Augh! The end is near! The end is near!*

And so here's my idea: I figure that the mental pressure of smashing into a book's end must squeeze something out of a writer. It must force them to cough up some sort of essential truth, because it's now or never.

With this in mind, I took the bus to the library and went into the fiction section and got a cart and chose a hundred novels at random from the shelves: potboilers, Nobel Prize winners, sci-fi, romance—everything. And I had a pile of coins and I went and photocopied the last two pages of each book and then I went to a coffee shop and read those hundred last pages looking for a common theme, and you know what? I found one. It's not in every book, but it's in most books. It's this: when a book ends, the characters are often moving either towards or away from a source of light— literally—like carrying a candle into a dark room or running a red light at an intersection or opening curtains or falling into a well or—this list goes on. I circled all the bits about light, and there's no mistaking it.

Makes you think, doesn't it?

Hope to see you soon, Roger.

Joan

Roger,

You've had a week to digest the custody results. I hope you're over it and not getting all maudlin or shaving your head into a Mohawk or some other crazy shit. I'm writing because of—oh Christ. A few days ago I was in the living room, picking up empty coffee cups, and I looked outside and there was this girl staring at the house—early twenties?—one of those Goth kids, pretty in a way, if she'd trowel off all the white junk on her skin. Why do kids do that these days?

I didn't give it much thought, but an hour later I looked out, and she was still staring. So I opened the door and asked her what she wanted, and she blushed (I'm assuming, beneath all the white junk) and mumbled something and sort of half ran, half walked away. I told Brian about her at dinner, and he said maybe it was some kid who used to live in this house before we moved in and wanted to see it again. I've done that myself, at the old family place in Steveston (which, BTW, is a stack of condominiums now), and I left it at that.

And then yesterday she was back out front. I didn't want to freak her out, and so I used my nice face and my nice voice and asked her if she'd like to come in. To be honest, I was curious about her, and I remember how happy it made me to see my family's old place.

She was iffy about coming inside, and I was about to close the door, but then she said yes and came forward. I asked her if she used to live here, and she said no. I asked if she was selling something, and she said no, so I got exasperated and asked her what she wanted. She asked if I was Joan, and I said yes, and—she was *so* nervous—I felt sorry for her, whoever she was.

So that's when she said she wanted to ask me about *you*, Roger. And I thought to myself, *Dear Lord, please don't tell me that he's now into Harajuku death princesses,* but she read my mind and said, "No, no, it's not like that. I'm not his girlfriend or stalking him or anything like that."

So I asked, "What are you here for, then?"

And she said, "To be honest, I was a little bit curious to see what you look like."

I gave her my icy stare—yes, the one you know very well—and she said, "Actually, I think Roger's in a bad way right now, and I don't know what to do or who else to go to."

I asked what sort of trouble, and she said, "Unhappy trouble—depression, maybe? Alcoholism? He hasn't been to work in a week."

I almost smiled. It was so sweet of her to believe that your disaster of a life was something brand new rather than something that had been playing itself out over many moons. She was so green that I asked her to sit.

I cleared away some of Zoë's toys, and we settled on the couch. I got nostalgic, almost, because she's obviously at that stage in her life where she's living in the secondhand shops and has rings of RIT Dye in shades of black and blue and maroon all around her bathtub. I didn't ask if she wanted coffee, because she was so fidgety. I simply told her I'd make herbal tea, but then I stopped myself and asked her if she wanted a glass of red wine. She said yes. It was two in the afternoon, but so what. Once a kid's in school, Roger, the days drag on forever, and I've never been much for housework. Drinking in the middle of the day must be a habit I picked up from you. Ha!

So young Bethany told me about knowing you from work at Staples. Roger, you are truly the mayor of Failure City. The punchline? She says you're in customer service. She also tells me you're working on a novel, and that you're well into it. That *does* come as a surprise: you actually started something? Snowballs in hell, and all of that. She said it's a "sophisticated adult drama" featuring a pair of rival authors. You? Creative? Artistic? All I remember is you doing one failed walk-on in the local North Shore Players production of *Same Time, Next Year*. All you had to do was knock on the door and hand the lead her ice bucket, and you fucked it up. And then you had your fling with her. Oops, did I mention your fling? I guess I did. Well, that's all in the past now, and I've got custody, so all's well that ends well.

Roger, Bethany's a sweet kid, and she's smart, but she's also young—young enough to think I might either care about you or want to help you. I told her that you go through "dark patches," but the moment the words left my mouth I regretted it, because girls love helping guys through dark patches and I don't want her lost in your orbit. I was then going to qualify my statement by saying, "There's no hope in trying to help him," but that would have been gasoline on the fire. So instead, I said, "He snaps out of these things almost like clockwork. You watch. He'll be right as rain within a few days." That cheered her up, and hopefully stripped your pity party of glamour.

Speaking of your pity party, Roger, get on with your life, okay? We're divorced. I got custody. Brian and I are marrying in three weeks. You're living in the past. You're living on *Fantasy Island*. So you're writing a novel—that's actually good news, for once. Park all your emotional crap there. Quit your loser job at Staples. Get a real job. Get sober. You've probably decided that nothing can happen until you "bottom out." You're battling for last place, and you're the only person in the competition.

On a purely technical matter, next weekend I'll be dropping off Zoë for her monthly three-hour visit. Do you want me to drop her off at your place, or do you want me to drop her off at a custody-visit hot spot like the aquarium? Your call.

You have my numbers and email.

J.

Glove Pond

Kyle paid the Chinese food delivery man, and Brittany carried the bags to the dining-room table, which had been dusted by Steve with several sweeps of a small throw rug.

Gloria then opened each grease-blotted delivery bag with wonder, as though it might yield gold, frankincense and myrrh. She made no effort to fetch cutlery or plates; Kyle went into the kitchen to find some. He rifled through the cutlery drawer, where he found chunky pieces of sterling silver dinnerware. The silver was so badly neglected that its surface was like the oil-caked and smeared concrete bay floors at a Mr Muffler franchise. *Jesus, these people are disasters*, he thought, looking for something, anything, that might be useable as serviettes. No paper towels. No tea towels. No cloth napkins. In the end, he found a three-week-old copy of a local shopping flyer, and around each knife/fork/spoon he folded a paper sheet. He carried these four set-ups out to the dining-room table.

"What are those?" asked Gloria.

"Set-ups."

"What's a set-up?"

"It's a restaurant term. Instead of placing a separate

napkin, fork, knife and spoon, you bundle them up in the back room and then simply put out one 'set-up' for each seat. It saves time."

Nobody commented on the fact that they were using newspaper sheets as napkins. Brittany removed her cutlery. "This is expensive stuff," she said. "Sterling."

"Wedding gifts," said Gloria.

"You could pawn each of these suckers for a few grand," said Kyle. "Your cutlery drawer is worth maybe forty grand."

Brittany said, "You could pay for a first-class trip around the world with just your serving spoons."

And here, dear reader, is where time froze for Steve and Gloria—where their perception of the universe stopped, leaving them in a not unpleasant dimensionless limbo. And then, like a small rose seedling emerging from beneath the winter snow to be kissed by the sun's love, both time and reality returned to the couple with a trickle. And then tiny acetylene bursts somewhere in their reptile cortexes were followed by walloping endorphin rushes and a moment of satori bliss.

"Kyle, we need plates," said Brittany.

Kyle went to fetch some while Steve and Gloria remained almost tasered with joy. Only after another minute did they return to full consciousness. They unwrapped their set-ups and began to poke into the contents of the takeout boxes and flats.

"Ooh!" said Gloria. "Moo goo gai pan. I love moo goo gai pan."

"No," said Steve. "You merely enjoy saying 'moo goo gai pan.'"

"And what if I do? Kyle, would you like some moo goo gai pan?" Gloria speared the largest, juiciest piece of chicken bathed in the foil tray amidst a flotsam of defeated mushrooms and vegetables.

"Sure," said Kyle.

Kyle was amazed at how much noise his putative hosts made while eating—their athletic slurping and brisk glottal vacuuming noises reminded him of nothing more than soft porn.

"So," said Brittany. "Where is your son right now?"

Steve and Gloria's forks stopped in mid-pounce. "Why do you ask?" asked Steve.

"I'm making conversation," said Brittany.

"Our son is a very special boy," said Gloria.

"Special indeed," Steve echoed.

Kyle assessed the data around him—the house frozen in time; Steve and Gloria's wrinkled skin; the absence of any evidence of human life under sixty—and pushing the limits of plausibility to the extreme, he asked, "Is he in college now, perhaps?"

Too quickly, Gloria said, "Yes. In college. Happy as a clam. Studying his brains out. Study, study, study."

"Can't believe how much he studies."

"His little noggin overflowing with knowledge."

"The brain is a marvellous thing."

"Dear," said Gloria to Steve, "there's no soy sauce here."

"There isn't, is there?"

"I'd better go into the kitchen and get some."

"I'll come with you."

Steve and Gloria got up from the table together and left the room.

Kyle looked at Brittany. "These people are mentally ill."

"It's all relative, Kyle. Maybe they're happy."

"They have no food in their kitchen."

"Few people do. They probably go to the deli once a day, like us."

"No, I mean no food whatsoever. A jar of pickle juice and a box of weevil-infested pancake mix older than the civil rights movement."

"You're exaggerating."

"I'm not."

"They appear well nourished."

"All they ingest is Scotch and gin."

"Keep your voice down. Maybe they can hear us."

"Are you going to eat that last bit of sweet-and-sour pork?"

"Be my guest."

Kyle ate the last piece of pork.

Toast 2: A High Seas Tale

11 Nov. 1893

Though the Vessel shakes with incessant nauseating rolls & pitches, my faith in a Promised Land free of grills and devices that scorch our tender farinaceous flesh shakes not. The ship's Captain, one Cornelius Jif—a hideous, unschooled poltroon of questionable agenda—has almost entirely reduced our daily ration of both cinnamon & sugar, this over and above last week's complete withdrawal of butter. Some of the fainter slices on board have swapped logic with salt water and have gone delirious from the cursed sogginess that is the perpetual enemy of we who travel on the Good Ship *Slice*, registered in Liverpool but flying the Canadian Dominion's flag (though only, one might add, when nearing crafts touting flags of nations hostile to America's open-loaf policy—a policy that promises shelter to those slices who, like myself and my family, sit huddled in babushkas & mite-choked rags 'neath the fo'c'sle, dreaming of lives free of staleness and the Grill).

Yesterday the Widow Bran surrendered Hope of reaching our destination and became a piteous sight on the aft deck, the angry gulls & skuas gobbling her fair carcass, their demonic cackles rousing Captain Jif from the afternoon round of *chemin de fer* he plays with the beweeviled ship's "Guests of Distinction": Lord Rye of Loafestershire, the Marchioness of Yeaste (said to have gone mad from a patch of mould on a raisin'ed slice) and the bellicose Herr Pumpernickel, heir to the fabled Knead fortune.

The only notion that gives us plain slices in steerage any hope is our Dream of one day inhabiting a land where freshness can live in peace, free of the perpetual mania engendered by the overbearing presence of cheeses, relishes & tuna mayonnaise.

But I neglect the most rousing of experiences, one that I must now here relate. We shored in Angra do Heroísmo, alongside the lava-domed Azorean coast, to restock a supply of durum wheat gone to mush from a leak in the prow—a leak caused by the unfortunate instance when Captain Jif—demented from a heady blend of liqueur-filled Yuletide chocolates and gambling wins—steered our vessel into a Turkish military ship, *Al Sheesh-Ke'h Bahb*. 'Twas a fearsome puncture that interrupted our almost unceasing prayers to Saint Gwynevere of Cruste,

Manuscript ends here.

Bethany

You're back.

With a bang!

Thank God.

And "Toast 2" was epic. To be honest, I've been going through Roger withdrawal. Things aren't the same around here without someone a bit older than the rest of us to whip us into shape. Since the incident of the stolen gum (the QuickTime securi-cam loop of the event went viral all over YouTube), everyone's paranoid and grim.

I hope you're feeling better. Eight days is a long time to have been away. It's Sunday today, but it feels more like a "generic" day—or rather, it feels like what days must have felt like before we invented the seven days of the week. Imagine waking up in the morning and not knowing what day of the week it is. What a strange sensation that must have been.

Hmmm—what day of the week is it? It's nothing. It's merely a day, a plain old day with no labels or meaning or anything.

Now go back further in time—to before humans named the four seasons. You'd go through life saying, "Gee, it's colder now—the cold weather usually follows a longish spot of good weather—and if memory serves me correctly, after a hundred more sleeps, the weather will be warming up again."

People must have gone absolutely crazy, not knowing for sure how long the cold and warm patches were going to last—so crazy that they had to make a Stonehenge, to be *sure*. Archaeologists are always wondering why cavemen dragged those huge stones halfway across England—well, come on! They were totally freaked out by not knowing what season it was.

It's slow at El Shtoopo—I think there are three big football games on TV, and that always empties out the place. Kyle's got the day off and is watching them at a friend's apartment. I'm killing time by walking up and down the aisles with a purposeful facial expression so that people don't interrupt me to ask questions. I've been doing this great big infinity loop of aisles 4 and 5 all day. QuickTime *that*.

La DeeDee is driving me nuts right now, so I signed on for some extra shifts. I can use the money either for Europe or for nursing school, though I don't know which it's going to be yet.

DeeDee read this factoid that said one person in ten thousand commits suicide. She figured that if she knows maybe a thousand people, there's still only a one in ten chance she'd know a suicide—but instead she knows eight people who've done it, and four of them were pretty close to her. So she's wondering if knowing many suicides is, in itself, an indicator of herself suiciding. Not that she would. She lacks the necessary confidence and self-esteem. She figures she'd somehow botch it and end up embarrassed and in a wheelchair.

You used to know the Deedster back before life crushed

her like a bug. Do you remember anything about her that might prod her in a productive direction again? Something? Anything?

At the moment, she spends her days leashed to a photocopier in a notary's office. It reminds me of those cartoons where there's a dog attached to a rope pegged in the middle of a yard. There's no hope of escaping, and she's lost the will to bark.

Depressing!

Bethany

Joan

Roger, now I know why your pal, Bethany, looked familiar. It was back at one of my Cancer Survival workshops. She was younger and chubbier, but it was her. Her aunt had breast cancer, and even near the end that woman was doing crafty things like appliquéing sequins onto denim pants. People who can achieve stuff even when they know they're goners amaze me, and when I think of Shakespeare keeping a skull on his desk while he wrote to remind him of his mortality? What a freak.

Anyway, Bethany's family used to argue *constantly*. The moment they walked into the room, everybody's T-cell count plummeted. And the noise they made! But Bethany always sat there dutifully and never got involved in the fray. If she recognized me from Survival workshops the other day, she didn't let on.

Hey, don't feed Zoë any sugar, not even fresh fruit. It sends her through the ceiling.

Brian will be back in exactly three hours to collect her. Enjoy your time together.

J.

Bethany

Mr. Rant was in today. I saw him arrive (it was pouring rain out, so he was doubly irritable; he made a big show of shaking out a Dole pineapple promotional collapsible umbrella with two broken spokes inside the doors). Kyle and I followed him, waiting for an outburst, and we weren't disappointed.

You know how every so often you get those guys in their fifties who walk up and down the aisles, whistling or humming tunelessly? There was one of those guys standing in Aisle 3-South, directly in Mr. Rant's way. The whistling guy seemed to be savouring Shtooples's premium selection of binders and Day-Timer products, humming that pointless, melody-free deedly-deedly music. Mr. Rant lost it: "What is *with* you people who whistle tunelessly? What is your problem! Why can't you either learn a proper song or simply keep your noise to yourself."

I piped up: "Are you finding everything you're looking for, sir?"

"Tell Mr. Microphone here to shut the heck up."

(Me, ingenuously) "Sorry?"

Mr. Rant ignored me and directed his anger at the Happy Whistler. "I used to think that you guys who whistle or hum tunelessly in public were simply idiots, but I think the truth is that you were all molested by your Boy Scout leader when you were eleven, and you haven't dealt with it yet, so instead you tunelessly whistle. Go get some therapy and leave the rest of us alone."

The Happy Whistler was obviously a therapy junkie. "Sir, you know, if you could keep your opinions to yourself, that would be really great."

Mr. Rant exploded: "*'That would be great'?* God, I *hate* that expression. It's passive-aggressive, it's condescending, and what you actually want to say is, 'I want you to keep your opinion to yourself,' except you're too chickenshit to say it flat out, so instead you say, 'That would be great.'"

The Happy Whistler went silent . . . a lone tumbleweed cartwheeled down Aisle 3-South.

Mr. Rant went for a hat trick: "Who designed the lighting in this place—the Nazis? Jesus, it makes everybody's skin look like eggs Benedict. And how many different kinds of blue ballpoint pen does the world need? I think a whole aisle dedicated solely to blue pens is an unhealthy thing for society and the environment." He looked at me. "Hey, I need a replacement toner cartridge for an HP LaserJet 1320. Where do I find one?"

Me: "Aisle 10-North, right-hand side."

As Mr. Rant walked away, he began whistling a note-perfect version of the "Mexican Hat Dance."

He made my day.

Roger

Hi DeeDee,

Bethany's at an age where she doesn't listen to anybody, so I don't think my opinion counts for squat here. But isn't it sick how she's ended up dead-ending here at Staples too, even though our lives are so different? *Laugh!* That was a joke.

DeeDee, hey, I got to thinking about you back when we were in school. I remember you used to paint—you did that big mural with melting clocks and an angry winged unicorn in the stairwell that led down into the smokehole. How about following up painting again?

Here's something: I've noticed that when you get older, you not only have a To-Do list but you could start making a Things-I-Used-To-Do list, too. Yesterday I found an old chunk of ski wax in the back of a drawer, and I could barely look at it because waxing my skis was a Thing I Used To Do—and then I finally took the wax out and threw it away. Which is all to say, if getting out the brushes and linseed oil freaks you out, I totally understand. It's strange how things leave you one by one, isn't it? Old friends. Enthusiasms. Energy. But Bethany inspires me to do something new. At the moment, writing keeps me sane.

R.

Glove Pond

Kyle was staring at his fork, Steve-like, trying to bend it by the use of his telekinetic rays. "You know, when we mentioned their kid, it was like we toasted Hitler at a bris or something."

"There aren't any photos of him anywhere in here," Brittany said.

"They don't seem like the kids type."

"And they've been gone for ten minutes now. How long can it take to find a bottle of soy sauce?"

"I didn't see any soy sauce in the fridge. Only that jar of pickle juice."

They poked at the cold remains of the Chinese food.

"What do you want to do?" asked Brittany.

"Maybe we should just get out of here and cut our losses. These people are living car crashes."

"Yes, but there has to be a reason they're such disasters. I'll go look for them. We can't leave without saying goodbye."

"Be my guest. In the meantime, I'll be here reading a—" Kyle reached over for a magazine on a nearby table "—June 1971 issue of *The New Yorker*."

Brittany went into the kitchen. It was empty, and the back door was open. She looked outside. The smell of rotting leaves was delicious, and she could see her breath in the porch light. On the back lawn, lit by a street lamp, two sets of footprints broke the frost. They led to the back alley. She followed them and, while doing so, caught her reflection in the window of a Ford Explorer parked in the rear lane. *So that's me.*

She shivered and looked at her feet, where there lay a Halloween residue of blown-up pumpkin chunks, dead fireworks and candy wrappers. She thought about her new makeup and the way she looked tonight. She thought of how rare it is that we catch glimpses of ourselves in mirrors—usually in public spaces—and see ourselves first as strangers see us. Then, upon recognizing ourselves, we're back to being stuck inside our bodies again, and back to having just a fuzzy sense of our being.

She carried on tracking the footprints until she lost them in a thicket of weeds.

Which way should I go?

Damn—it's that interior voice again, never shutting up.

She strained to hear Steve and Gloria, but all she heard was an electrical humming sound. She looked up and saw transformers atop the utility poles. She had never noticed transformers before, but now she saw that they were as pervasive in the urban world as street lights, parked cars and trees. *Why are they everywhere? Aside from simply being called transformers, what do they actually* do? *What do they transform? How do they do it?*

She stopped and huffed out a breath, and it hung there in the cold as though in a museum's showcase. She was cold.

And then she heard what sounded like small drums beating a few backyards over. In spite of the chill, she went to investigate. Peering over the fence in a neighbour's yard, she saw Steve and Gloria under the moonlight, stealing armloads of plastic children's toys—a Fisher-Price plastic scooter, a hula hoop, a red plastic pony-shaped rocking toy and other coloured vinyl forms she couldn't make out. They were so loaded down with stolen swag that in silhouette they resembled deformed Christmas trees.

Brittany ducked behind a shed as the couple began heading back to their own house. The plastic toys, bouncing against each other, sounded like bamboo wind chimes. It was a pretty sound, blameless and kind.

Brittany followed. At the back door, Steve removed a key, and he and Gloria took the load of stolen toys into the basement. This was her chance to get back into the house unnoticed. She darted back to sit beside Kyle.

Steve and Gloria ever so casually came into the dining room. "The soy sauce was a little bit hard to find," said Gloria, "But voilà!" With the air of someone producing difficult-to-obtain food—fugu livers, say, or absinthe—she dropped a six-ounce bottle of La Choy soy sauce on the table, a sauce so old that it had turned solid inside the bottle.

"Soy sauce. I hope the food hasn't gone cold."

Glove Pond

Steve and Gloria had hastily grabbed a series of sweaters and overcoats from the alcove beside the rear kitchen door and were trying to don gardening gloves caked with brittle summer dirt.

"Bloody guests—they're never anything but trouble. First they arrive, and then they sit there and eat your food."

"*You* invited them. And it's been so many years now without guests."

"Well, I *had* to invite them. You know how interdepartmental politics are. Everything was going just fine until that young maverick, Fraser, from Humanities brought in his ergonomically correct Balans chair to meetings. I've been out of kilter ever since. And then I turn around, blink, and suddenly I'm railroaded into having this Falconcrest idiot here for dinner."

"Balans chairs? Those are those chairs with no backs and all the pressure is on your knee—"

"Yes, yes."

"I saw a PBS documentary on them. They'll soon be replacing every chair on earth."

"Wretched things. God, I hate the present."

They stepped out into their backyard, the frost-covered

lawn altering the night air in a way that made Steve feel as if all sounds were moving away from his ears.

Gloria asked, "What are we going to do now?"

"Same thing as last time."

"Last time we did this it was summer. I'm cold."

"So am I."

"Let's just hurry, then."

The couple walked down the rear alley, peeking into successive yards in pursuit of something decidedly specific.

"There?" asked Gloria, pointing to a white plastic pony with a pink fringe and a purple tail.

"Gloria, Kendall was a *boy*."

"I'm not stupid, Steve. I just thought it looked . . . cheerful."

"Don't think about it too much, Gloria. You know it'll only make you hurt."

"Steve, I keep waiting for that to change. But it never does."

"It doesn't. It won't."

"How can you be sure?"

"Because I've read everything I can about it. The important books, the unimportant books. Even an article in *The New Yorker*. The most you can ever expect is that you'll simply get used to it." Steve stopped looking into other yards and looked only at his toes.

Gloria stopped and said, "But it's been so long now, and I'm not used to it. How could a person possibly become used to it?"

"Don't ask *me*, Gloria. I'm not there yet, and let's change the subject. It never goes anywhere but down."

Gloria nodded towards a yard. "I see some toys over there."

"Jesus, those people must have triplets. Look at all that plastic."

"Let's just do this quickly, Steve."

"Right."

Glove Pond: Kyle

While everyone was gone, Kyle had used the opportunity to investigate the secret life of Steve.

That turkey-cocking fraud must have an office here somewhere.

He found the guest bathroom with its white sink coated in dust. In the soap dish were some cracked and splintering hotel soaps from the distant past. Beside the toilet was the first chapter of *Love in the Age of Office Superstores*. Kyle was astounded: *First he steals my manuscript, and then he leaves it beside the toilet?*

Outside on the hallway's flocked walls hung framed yellowed fox hunting prints above a demi-lune side table on which rested far more objects than it was ever meant to hold: a dusty wicker basket full of dusty keys, the locks they opened long since forgotten; five unmated men's gloves; middens of neglected bank statements and bills; piles of half-sucked white Scotch mints; a heap of injured reading glasses and sunglasses; a dozen or so cosmetic products that had evidently fallen into Gloria's disfavour; plus various hardware-like objects whose function was unclear to Kyle.

At the hallway's end were two doors. One led into a parlour area, where, in a corner, sat a small black-and-white Philco TV, sans cable hookup, its antenna snapped in two. The room beside this was, *bingo*, Steve's office. It reminded Kyle of *New Yorker* cartoons of offices in which flapper-era plutocrats chased their melon-breasted secretaries in circles around a large, document-cluttered desk lit by a brass banker's light with a green glass shade. Closer inspection revealed a carpeting wear pattern from door to desk. A leather sofa groaned beneath its predictable load of yellowed newspapers and magazines. Kyle picked up a paper dated from a previous era ("President Touts 'Information Superhighway'; Naysayers See Only Speed Bumps"), and the paper crumbled in his hands. He rubbed a finger along the sofa's back and found that the dust in this particular room had fused with decades' worth of pipe tobacco smoke to form a greasy, borderline explosive substance not unlike the Alberta tar sands. He tried rubbing the molasses-y substance off on the ledge of a bookshelf beside the door, only to accrue more noxious goo. He scraped his finger off on the bottom of his shoe.

Say what you will about the old monster, he did manage to complete five novels, Kyle thought as he moved closer to Steve's desk, looking for evidence of the sixth, the one that allegedly took place in an office superstore.

Kyle sat down in Steve's baronial leather desk chair. He expected a bit of bounce, but instead his coccyx slammed neatly into the chair's solid base, its interior foam latex stuffing having long ago encrusted into brittle yellow sand that dribbled out from frayed cushion corners.

Kyle looked at the desk before him. Where to start? He searched for anything that resembled a manuscript, but saw only unopened bills, interdepartmental memos, nude sunbathing magazines from the early 1970s, and stacked phone books that became successively older as one descended through the strata. There was a pizza box in the midst of this, and Kleenexes stuffed into available nooks and crannies. To the right sat an ashtray the size of a hubcap, filled with a powder keg volume of ash, burnt matchsticks and scorched wads of spearmint chewing gum. Several pipes rested around its edge.

Kyle opened the main drawer and found a couple of empty packages of gum and two old passports, the more recent of the two having expired in 1979. There was a menu from a Greek takeout restaurant, clipped newspaper articles on the theme of colon health, and dozens of empty matchbooks dating from the era when steak, jumbo lobsters, A-framed buildings and anything tiki were considered the peak of dining sophistication. There was no computer or typewriter, but by the window, leaning into the room's corner beneath its requisite nicotine wash, sat a 1980 Daewoo Heavy Industries OfficeWrite 2300 Word Processing System. Below it was an unopened carton of dot matrix tractor-edged paper. The corner was an eloquent haiku for yet another past era, one in which democracy remained under constant threat from female Soviet weightlifters and sleek East German technology.

He opened the topmost of two large drawers on the desk's right-hand side. It contained mostly empty tins of pipe tobacco, plus framed desktop photos, their standing mechanisms folded inwards, the group of them stacked atop each other. Some were ancient, and their subjects unidentifiable. But there was one of a pubescent Gloria atop a hunter with a braided mane, and one of a post-pubescent Gloria clipped from a *Town & Country*–style magazine: *Who will nab this year's jewel in the crown, the delightful Gloria Harrington?* There was a shot of movie-star-handsome Steve and Gloria sharing a daiquiri at San Francisco's Top of the Mark. But, as with everywhere else in the house, there was no evidence of any remotely current time period. If Steve and Gloria had a child of any age, Kyle had yet to locate the evidence.

Kyle closed the top drawer and reached for the handle of the bottom drawer. It occurred to him that in this drawer lay the secret of Steve—if one was only to open it, in a flash, the reason why both Steve and Gloria were disasters would be revealed.

He was about to pull it open when he heard thumps from the basement.

Bethany

Hi Roger,

I guess I'd better confess that I actually know your ex-wife—Joan. Does that weird you out? She was in my aunt's cancer survivor group, and I remembered her because of the code word: "spleen." You're right, a spleen is a strange thing—we technically don't need one, but maybe spleens are kept in our bodies in case we mutate or evolve, and if we grow wings or tentacles we need to have the spleen in place in order for them to work. That's my theory.

I don't know if Joan would remember me. That was back before I decided to win the heart of Johnny Depp through the inventive application of scary makeup. Also, my family overshadowed me at cancer meetings. Imagine a group of people even more annoying than mimes, with the added bonus of loud, grating speech and no sense of manners or propriety. That would be us. Mom and her ex-husband were in this war over who could do a better job of caring for Aunt Paulette (long story), and the caring portion got lost along the way. Cancer is, among many other things, a spectator sport.

Like you need a depressing letter like this.

How many times have you heard the expression about cancer patients, "They were never sick a day in their life, and suddenly, bang, they're gone"? Well, it turns out that being sick is actually good for you. Colds and flus are like these constant refresher courses that teach your body how to combat cancers when they first occur. Some people think that the moment you get your diagnosis you should run out to the children's coloured plastic ball pit at IKEA and coat your body with kiddy germs and get as sick as you can. While you're in the process of fighting the colds and flus, the cancer gets taken out with the trash. Cool, huh? You might think this sounds stupid, but after sixty years of antibiotics, we're right back to maggots as the best way to get rid of dead tissue.

This was all to say that I can put a face on your ex, and isn't the world a small place?

I'm on the cash register until closing tonight and am going to be one grouchy little Goth at the end of it. Something about Wednesdays makes people cruel.

The *Glove* rocks. Keep it up.

B.

PS: Okay, I confess, I went to Joan's house. She was easy to find. Google. I was worried about you—you vanished, dammit!—but I promise I didn't come across as a stalker or a psycho, and I've seen enough nasty divorce shit in my life to know how to avoid accidentally inflaming people. So the encounter went smoothly, and you don't have to worry that I messed your life up. She was nice, and didn't say anything bad about you, and I was *so* worried about you, Roger.

There.

I feel better. But, Roger, you have a beautiful daughter you almost never mention. That's pretty great!

DeeDee

Roger,

I've been doing some thinking, and what do you know about Kyle? It's great that Bethany's got a guy, but . . . okay, here's what's confusing me: he's way too good-looking to be working at a pit like Staples (sorry, Roger). He seems to like Bethany, but—and this is so cruel, and I am a bad, bad mother—isn't he really way out of her league? This from me, the thrice-divorced mess. But you know I have a point. Is he dumb? He doesn't strike me as a druggie. Maybe pot, because he's pretty mellow. Why couldn't Bethany fall for some pimpled stick figure at a record store? That's what I always had planned for her. But then, I don't know if record stores still exist. Do they? Maybe that's where my plan went wrong.

Okay, there was a triggering incident. Kyle was over at our place and we were watching TV. He opened the fridge door to look for something to eat or drink, looked at what was inside, and then closed the door and came back into the living room like he'd never gone near the fridge. He didn't make a face or anything. He said nothing, as if he'd never looked inside it. So I got up (we were watching more reality crap, what else?) and looked for myself, and in my head I was seeing Kyle, raised by a succession of trophy wives, each of them primping in front of a mirror and selecting their daily sunglasses, and each of them saying words to the effect of, "There's tons of expensive, nutritious food in the fridge, Kyle, but if you go to someone else's house, for the love of God, don't allow them to feed you crap. Otherwise, you'll end up like them."

Our fridge was filled with fatty, sugary crap, and no wonder I'm turning out the way I am. No wonder Bethany's going in the same direction. Why couldn't she have been a vegetarian? That might have whipped me into shape. But no, when this Goth thing began, we were at the IGA and she asked the butcher how to order blood by the quart. It was one of those few moments in life when you literally freeze. And now she's dating way too high up the food chain and I'm at my wits' end. Who is this guy? What does he want?

If you ever tell Bethany I wrote this, I will kill you.

DD

Glove Pond

"The soy sauce has mummified," said Kyle.

"What do you mean?" asked Gloria.

He shook the La Choy bottle. "It's turned into a little black hockey puck, bonded onto the bottom." He handed the bottle to Gloria.

"It needs to be warmed up a bit is all. I'll go put it in the double boiler for a few minutes. It'll melt in no time."

"There was no soy sauce in the fridge or cupboards," said Kyle, under his breath. "I looked."

"Of course not. This bottle was part of our honeymoon gift from Daddy's lawyer. It was a Japanese home cooking kit, and I've been keeping it down in the nice cool basement so it would be fresh for a festive occasion such as this."

"How long have you been married?" Brittany asked.

"Thirty-six years."

"It's okay," said Brittany. "I don't need soy sauce."

"Me neither," said Kyle.

"Let me see that bottle," said Steve. He opened it and began digging at its contents with a disposable chopstick. "It's not hard," he said. "It's granular." Steve sprinkled some soy shavings onto the cold, oily glacier that was once moo goo gai pan, and then ate a forkload.

"Delicious. A good soy sauce is like a good wine. Gets better with age."

"So, Kyle," said Gloria, unaware that she was batting her lashes, "is your family literary?"

"Literary?"

"Do they, you know, read books? Are they like me, for example—and live for nothing but art and music and masterful writing?"

"Kyle doesn't like discussing his family," said Brittany.

"Why not?" asked Steve.

"I don't think it's anyone's business," said Kyle.

Brittany said, "Kyle thinks his family is nothing but a collection of emotionally frozen, passive-aggressive hillbillies."

"Really?" asked Steve.

"That's not true," said Kyle.

"But it is," Brittany said, "and never discussing them won't make it untrue." She looked at Gloria. "Our place is like your place. No family photos anywhere. Not even stuck to the fridge with a magnet. When I try to ask about his family, the subject gets changed."

"Gloria," said Kyle, "tell me more about your upcoming role as Lady Windermere in the local dinner theatre production of *Lady Windermere's Fan*."

"It's the lead role, you know."

"It must be difficult."

"She can't remember her lines," said Steve.

Gloria spun around to Steve. "That's not true! One doesn't *remember* lines, Steve. One *internalizes* them. One doesn't rattle off lines like an idiot savant. There must be a soul and music to them. Please pass me some Scotch." Gloria poured.

"I had to memorize half of human knowledge to become a surgeon," said Brittany. "But I could never memorize a script. And *Lady Windermere's Fan* is a long play with complex nuances."

Kyle asked, "How *do* you remember your lines? Do you have any techniques?"

"I try to read the lines and have the emotions behind them fill my body."

"Hooey," said Steve. "You have no technique. Trying to get memories to stick to your brain is like trying to get Ping-Pong balls to stick to a brick wall."

"I'll make a very good Lady Windermere," said Gloria. "I will."

Brittany changed the subject. "Before you went to fetch the soy sauce, we were discussing your son," she said. "The one in college."

"Ah, yes." Steve and Gloria spoke in unison.

"What's his name?" Kyle asked.

Steve and Gloria looked as though they were deciding whether to accept a plea bargain.

"Yes," said Brittany. "I bet you chose a good name."

Gloria sipped her Scotch and Steve idly scraped more flecks of mummified soy sauce from its diseased flask.

There was a silence.

Finally, Steve said, "Kendall. His name is Kendall."

Gloria looked at him as if to say, *Really?*, but quickly snapped to and said, "Yes, young Kendall. Such a good son."

c/o YHA London—Hampstead Heath Hostel
4 Wellgarth Road
London, England

VIA FEDEX

Hi, Roger.
Surprise! I'm in jolly olde London. I made the jailbreak!
Farewell, Shtooples! Sorry I didn't say goodbye to you. I
didn't want to make a big deal out of leaving. Getting my
passport took a week, and I talked myself in and out of this
maybe fifty times while I was waiting for it. Was there a
new chapter of *Glove Pond* to read—or a diary entry? I'll
have missed it. Sorry.

It's *great* here, Roger, art and beauty and music and
stuff everywhere—I feel like Gloria, which is scary—except
every time I look at the price on anything I faint. How can
these people afford to live in their own country? We got
here a week ago and are staying in this hostel in a place
called Hampstead, which is where Wallace and Gromit
would live if they were here: nice little stone houses, and
behind every door I can clearly sense the presence of various kinds of exotic cheddars. All they eat in this country is

sandwiches—the kind you got in your lunch box in school, cut diagonally and sold in sets of two inside vacuum-packed containers at corner stores and train stations. I bet even the car dealerships and kidney dialysis centres here sell them. It's all we're eating because it's all we can afford. By "we," I mean Kyle and me. There was a, well, er, uh . . . a scene before I went to the airport. Poor DeeDee. She has it in her head that I'm throwing my life away and that I'm going to end up like her unless I go back to school. Right. As if I want the rest of my life to be nothing but watching TV reruns with a mild headache. Not if I can help it. I had a bit of money stashed away, and Kyle sold his Mom's OxyContins and a few other things, and tiddly-dee-dee, pip-pip, we're in England!

Highlights:

We saw a Punch and Judy show in the park, which was depressing because it's November and cold and cloudy, and the kids are all in school, so I don't know what the puppeteers were thinking—unless it was only a practice run. But good Lord, it's nothing but wife beating. Have you ever seen one of these? They obviously didn't have women's shelters in the Middle Ages. What a disaster to have been born before 1980.

We've gone to a few pubs, and they're actually not as pubby as I'd hoped. I'd been expecting sawdust on the floors, crusty factory workers playing darts and an eccentric woman in a tweed coat sitting in the corner with a duck on her lap. Instead, everything is digital, high-tech and beautifully lit, and when you order a beer, it's like being at Lord Twindlebury's beer smorgasbord. It's all so deluxe and polished, even the dives, though people smoke here and every night before bed I have to rinse out my hair.

Oh! I had jet lag for the first time, and it was almost fun—it made things that were weird to me feel even weirder—enhanced. It's like MSG.

There aren't nearly as many girls here my age who are into pursuing Johnny Depp as a husband. Everybody's so rich-looking. And how can somebody be rich in a place where everything is so insanely expensive? The people my age all have their money act together. I'm feeling a bit freakish right now and may tone down my look a notch. Or maybe I'll amp it up. No idea.

Enough already. I have yet to meet Count Chocula and his jewel-encrusted dildo from the Crusades.

Keep working on *Glove Pond*. Kyle is jealous I'm writing you, so maybe I'll write you more than ever.

Ta for now,

B.

PS: As you can see, I've moved up in the world and am using FedEx. There's a storefront down the street here in Hampstead and, even better, in my address book I've got the account number of Mom's creepy boss, who stuck his tongue in my ear at their office do three years ago. He's a perv, and I'm not going to let it wreck my life, but I'm certainly going to use his account while I'm here. ;)

Joan

Roger, the wedding is this weekend, and rather than throw five hundred bucks into the shredder and have my lawyer draft you something, I'm sending you this myself instead. I know the past years have been rough on you, but they've been rough on me, too—and *I* don't count, it's Zoë who counts, and frankly, this wedding is mostly about Zoë having some nice pictures in her head when she thinks of the word "marriage." I'd have been quite happy to go to the counter where they issue dog tags at city hall and fill out a form and have it done with. So yes, I'm asking you not to rent the Fuji Blimp and print scary shit on its digital sign board, or rent a WWI Sopwith Camel with a crude message trailing after it, or hire a jet to skywrite a skull and bones over the church. Please leave us alone and get on with something else. Okay?

I want to confirm that Zoë's coming with us on the trip to Hawaii after the service (you'll notice I didn't use the word "honeymoon"? Honeymoons, like Trix, are for kids), so your three hours with her will be postponed for two weeks.

That's about it.

Oh, I forgot to remind you that you're the one who had the affair with the cheesy actress in the local dinner theatre production of *Same Time, Next Year*, and that's what started this whole ball rolling.

Joan

PS: I never heard again from young Lily Munster who showed up on my doorstep a few weeks ago.

PPS: It kills me that you won't be making child support payments any more, but I'm remarrying, so that's the law. Think of all the extra beer you can now drink by yourself in your basement apartment. Woohoo! Life's a blast.

Bethany

c/o YHA London—Hampstead Heath Hostel
4 Wellgarth Road
London, England

VIA FEDEX

Hi, Roger.
You'll notice I'm using paper and pen again. Screw email. I want to keep our noble storyteller's tradition alive. Kyle is already homesick and lives in the nearby Internet café, which is beside a kebab restaurant, so it all smells like grease and those spices that normal people buy and put in their spice rack but never use from one decade to the next. Question: Have you ever looked closely at a donair? Answer: Don't.

It's been ten days now, and I think I might actually be burning out on London. We spend all our time in subways and standing on corners looking at maps and feeling like hillbilly tourists. Question: Roger, have you ever felt depressed? Answer: Pigeons. Those poor creatures and the lives they lead. I . . . don't want to go into it. If London is a meal, then pigeons are the parsley on top of it, except instead of being green and crisp, they're grey and hobbling and missing toes, and while they may appear to be technically cute, they also appear to be riddled with disease and mites.

We've been trying to meet locals, but we're citizens of London's weird parasitic shadow economy. It's composed of people like us who have the notion that we can use our grandmother's EU birth certificate to scam our way into genuine European jobs. The only people we're likely to encounter are fellow tribe members, none of whom are locals. Mostly they're foreigners our age with either no job or a sketchy one, who go to these parties that go on all night. It's dawning on me that there's not much I'm equipped to do for a living—either here or back home—and so all I have is my attitude and my skin, which has not been touched by the sun for over five years. Today I walked past a Staples on Oxford High Street and broke out laughing: they're identical to the ones back home.

Do you think Kyle could ever be a provider?

As I write this, he's emailing everybody he ever went to school with or worked with to fish for more emails in return. I don't think he's used to being uncomfortable—this in the man I love. He's had two stepmoms and he milked them both for all the buy-my-silence money he could—and if you factor in how totally guilty his real mom and his father felt, you can imagine the shower of comfort and trinkets that has rained down on him since the cradle. Was that last sentence too long? He's used to being a prince, and here he's merely another lame tourist.

Well, Bethany, Roger thanks you for the champagne flute full of negative energy you just hucked into his face.

Sorry about that, Roger.

There are things here that I like! The Museum of Natural History. A small display case filled with ultra-deep sea creatures was worth the admission alone—tiny, monstrous personalities frozen into animal shapes. The museum had a recreation of a dinosaur's nest, and somebody had put extinguished cigarette butts in it, and it was like that *Far Side* cartoon of dinosaurs smoking, with the caption, "Why dinosaurs became extinct."

But enticing golden boy to show a whiff of adventurous spirit is proving hard to do. If nothing else, I want to take the Chunnel to France. I can dream. The hostel is really wearing on me. I think I'm one-point-six years too old to really care about the stuff most of the hostellers care about (cheap beer; cheap tickets; an even cheaper hostel), and even something simple like doing laundry takes roughly the same amount of time, energy and money as buying and assembling a large IKEA bookshelf. And then I walk around the city and see the amazing houses people live in, and I look at my own life and I feel like a hamster.

How are Steve and Gloria? Have we met Kendall yet? And where does Gloria get tonic for her gin? I think that's a plot point you missed. Maybe her family set her up with a beverage endowment. I've met a few trust-fund kids here, and I can already tell that there's nothing a fucked-up rich family won't do with their money.

Kyle is ready to go. We're headed to Piccadilly to meet up with some deejay we met at a party in Wimbledon two nights ago. The previous sentence sounds way more glamorous than it is.

Write me a letter, why don't you? Paper is more old-fashioned and warped, even when sent FedEx.

My email address is blackchandelier@gmail.com in case you're feeling modern and lazy. I check the address daily.

Bye, Roger.
Ta!
B.

DeeDee

Roger,

I came to Staples but it was your day off. They wouldn't give me your home address, your phone's unlisted, and you have no Google existence. Are you a Unabomber or something?

Bethany left with that wretch, Kyle. She told me she was going to England the morning before the afternoon flight, and I botched it and screamed all the things you're not supposed to scream, which gave her the moral high ground and allowed her to slip into dignified silence mode—which inflamed me more. When numbnuts came to pick her up, I threw the Braun coffeemaker at him from the balcony. But what—I was supposed to let her run away and do something stupid, and say nothing? What sort of mother would I be if I did that?

What the hell is she going to do in England? England? Who goes to *England*? High school choirs, soccer hooligans, tea salesmen and pansies. She said she's going to Europe for half a year and she's going to get a job there because her father's mother was born in Brussels—some sort of European visa boondoggle. Yeah, right. They're going to smoke pot, meet losers, sit on trains and eat junk food. That's all young people do there, along with fucking around. I did the Europe thing once, except I had no illusions about what it was about. Sex and drugs. Period.

Oh God, I'm jealous. And I'm utterly sick with worry, though I think Bethany could hold her own in the gutters of Hanoi if she had to. I'm so lonely I can barely think. I got a terse little mini-email from her today, and it was way worse than hate mail. "Mom. I'm fine. Relax."

She's there with *somebody else*, and even if that somebody is that scheming prick, at least she has somebody.

Has she written you? Is she writing you? I hope she is. I think it's good she has one adult in her life she can talk to. I want you to grill all those twerps there at Staples and find out what you can about Kyle. Does Bethany email them? Did she get a job? Does she hate every minute of it and plan on coming home soon?

Sorry, I didn't ask you if you were fine. Bethany said you didn't have the flu, but that you were depressed about something, and she didn't know what, but now you're back at work. How is your novel coming? How can you concentrate on something that takes so long to do?

I'm off to a doctor's appointment.

I appreciate whatever help you can give me.

Bye.
DD

Roger

DeeDee,

I'm not going to act as a go-between between a mother and her daughter. Let Bethany enjoy Europe. She's hasn't written me, but she also isn't the type to do freaky, crazy shit like we might have done in the seventies. Yes, she wears vampire makeup, but it's only makeup—it's make-believe— it's something to tide her over until something more real comes along. As for Kyle? He's a blank. A generic good-looking kid with zero ambition and grades that stink—why else would he be working at Staples at, what, twenty-four? Kyles like him will be selling cellphone packages at twenty-five, and by thirty they'll have their shit together enough to get a pickup and start a half-assed gardening service, and by forty they'll be in coke or meth rehab, but by then our Kyle will be almost two decades out of Bethany's picture. Whatever is between them, it's not going to last. You know it. I know it. So relax.

Today has been strange for me. To be honest, I miss my mother, which is something I never experienced when she was alive. Missing that ~~mean spirited, sour~~ judgmental old battle-axe is the *last* thing I would have expected, but today I was in an ATM lineup at the bank, and there was this woman in front of me who, from behind, was the spitting image of my mother—the same hair colour and cut, and she held herself the way my mother did, her whole body bent in an arc. And she was wearing yellow ochre, my mother's favourite colour. I had no idea a simple colour could mean so much. Anyway, for the first thirty seconds I was looking at this woman from behind, I didn't make the connection that it wasn't my mother or that my mother was dead. I felt as if I were a teenager again, and I'd bumped into her there in the bank, and the moment she turned around and saw me I was going to catch shit for something I'd done wrong. But then the woman moved, and it wasn't my mother, and I felt socked on the jaw. My body felt all boneless and my eyes teared up, and then I got mad because the last thing I want in my life right now is more *grief* or *memories*. I'm sick of everything leaving my life, and nothing new ever coming my way.

What keeps me going right now, DeeDee, is the notion that, stripped of any form of protective coating—of stupidity, of youth, of ignorance, of money—of anything that might allow me to delude myself, I still manage to hang in there and go to that wretched Staples and stack the reams of twenty-pound bond paper and direct customers to the Maxwell House coffee promotional kiosk. It's a wonder I don't arrive one morning and drive through the front windows in my car, taking out as many people as I can in one grand, glorious gesture.

Strike that. I'm not a psycho. If anything, I'll probably drink too many vodka Breezers and get mellow out by the back door, where the girls take their smoke breaks. Guys don't smoke any more. Notice that?

It's fun when I'm buzzed and throwing tennis balls to my dog, Wayne. The girls get such a kick out of it, and for a ten-minute window they can think of me as a real person.

Here are some passing thoughts. Imagine looking up at the moon and seeing it burning.

Imagine seeing the grocery store's checkout girl grow horns.

Imagine growing younger instead of older.

Imagine feeling more powerful and more capable of falling in love with life every new day instead of being scared and sick and not knowing whether to stay under a sheet or venture forth into the cold.

Break time is over. I'm training to work as an aisle associate in the Personal Digital Assistant aisle. That's "PDA" in our high-tech world here.

Roger

Roger

DeeDee,
I thought over the letter I sent two days ago and realized it was a depressing pile of crap and you need something like that like you need a hole in the head. So I'm sending you these daisies—at least, that's what the picture on the screen showed. I was going to throw in a little silver Mylar balloon with "Sorry" printed on it, but that might make you retch. I promise not to write such a depressing letter again.

Roger

To Bethany
c/o YHA London—Hampstead Heath Hostel
4 Wellgarth Road
London, England
VIA your secret FedEx number

Bethany . . . first things first: write your mother, okay? She's going nuts worrying about you. Enough said.

Next: I'm glad you told me you visited Joan. The last while has been kind of rough and, yeah, I'm having trouble these days, but Joan isn't what you'd call a fountain of sympathy. I can make up all the excuses I want, but the fact is, I merely lie in my bed in the morning and don't get out. Especially at this time of year. I ask you, why do we even bother having wakefulness? Dreams are way more interesting than real life, and in dreams you never have to get out of bed. For that matter, why does life bother going forward? No matter what organism you look at . . . an amoeba or an elk or whatever, it does everything it can to advance itself—it tries to not be killed, it tries to mate, it tries to not be eaten. What's the nature of this divine computer program that drives everything to go *forward*? Why doesn't DNA sometimes say to itself, "You know what? I'm tired of this survival shit. I think I'm going to pack it in. It ends here."

Guess who had to put up the Christmas displays this year? You guessed it. God, how fucking depressing. I feel like Mr. Rant. Think about it: who cares a flying fuck whether or not an office superstore wishes them a seasonal greeting? I find it offensive. I'd prefer if, in December, a large office supply corporation held a "Just Pretend It's February" promotional campaign. If a company did that, I'd camp out in their stores all through December. The most seasonal thing you'd see would be a cardboard groundhog on a fake Groundhog Day reminding you to upgrade your PC's memory card.

BTW, in the new year I'm going to be a PDA Associate. I took a three-day training seminar taught by what appeared to be an eleven-year-old who had no social skills; welcome to the twenty-first century. Everyone understood what the guy was saying but me, and *man*, did I feel old, so to make myself feel less old, I forced myself to memorize the entire PDA user manual to learn all there is to know about these suckers. I can now tell you how to program one into sending your mother a 6:00 a.m. wake-up call on her 117th birthday—assuming you wanted to. I truly wish to see the shock on everyone's faces when I effortlessly show users how to flip between the Gregorian calendar and the calendar used by the Japanese imperial family. I know they're all waiting for me to crash and burn, but they're not going to get that satisfaction. Using a PDA is easier than I thought it would be, and it's fun and gives me something to do when I can't force myself out of bed.

I sound like I'm in a worse space than I am. I'm only mad at the world.

You can't hear Wayne howling. He's got some kind of bug and won't eat properly. I'm probably going to take him to the vet this morning, which will sorely tick off Fearless Leader—we're understaffed today, Dell Day, no less. Oodles of shit is going to hit a massive fan blade.

Fun sending a FedEx . . . never done it before. I feel like a confident industry professional, and it's great having the drop-off box outside the store's front door. It's like we have our own private mail system.

Don't happy, be worry. Oops . . . other way around.

R.

Zoë

Hi, Dad.
I really love ~~Mowie~~ Maui and today I found a clam. We had a sWordfish for dinner last night. I have my own room and it has free soap. I have to go now.

Zoë

The Epke Family

At this, the most special time of the year,
it brings great pleasure to wish you and yours
the best for the holiday season.

Dear Friends,
Excuse the impersonal "mass mailing" of the family

newsletter, but email is so mechanical and I don't want to handwrite a hundred Christmas cards!

Chances are you were at our wedding mere weeks ago. Joan has made an honest man out of me. Our honeymoon was a blast, and young Zoë overcame her fear of waves and was a paddle-boarding fiend on our Maui "Wowie" adventure. Returning to the "real world" was pretty darn hard!

The new house is coming along well, although we lost momentum fixing it up in spring and there are still several walls with unpainted plaster patches. One room we will certainly have to fix up is the nursery because, yup, there's a "bun in our oven"! Expect big things early next summer! And Joan wants to make sure I tell everybody that she's quit smoking, but only until fall, when she promises to be lighting up again. Between then and now, I'm sure we'll be having some pretty energetic debates on that topic!

On the work front, all goes well. I've landed gigs on ten new productions, three of which were renewed for two seasons, but I don't want to jinx things and am trying to work hard and earn what was a great opportunity to show the company all I've got!

Everyone is in good shape, especially Dad, who had his angio in September and is now 110 percent. He's discovered fleece jackets and likes to walk a mile every day. What next—marathons!?!?!

Thank you to everyone for giving us such great wedding presents, and for making our wedding day the magical day it was. Let's hope that next year is as good as this year.

Greetings from Brian, Joan and Zoë

Bethany

VIA FEDEX

Hi, Roger.

I hope Wayne is better. He'd love England—dogs all over the place, and they're darned sophisticated dogs too. Honestly, to see some of them, you'd think they read *Elle Decoration* magazine and do yoga.

We met two guys from home—the exact same sort of guys Kyle would have met at a sports bar on Marine Drive—and so we have a posse, but they're jockish and not very fun, so when they're around I feel like a fifth wheel. Kyle is not quite the sweet young thing who once filled Ziploc bags with trail mix for me.

Moan, moan, moan, grumble, grumble, grumble. When is the European magic going to kick in and rock my world? When am I going to befriend Count Chocula? The only people I ever seem to meet here are twenty-three-year-old Australians named Tracy who got crabs in Prague and who have voices like the buzzer they use on game shows when you get the answer to a question wrong.

Remember I wrote you awhile back about DeeDee telling me about meeting strangers in airport bars and spilling your life story to them because you know you'll never see them again? That's actually what I'm hoping for here. Is that sick? Kyle should be the one I'm telling everything to. So I feel a bit disloyal. But I wish Kyle would revel a bit more in the fact that we're in *a country that is not the one he grew up in*. The only time he ever gets stoked is when he finds things or places or people that remind him of home. I now like to walk around by myself, mostly. When we got here, K and I were spending *all* of our time together, but I don't think you see things properly when you're with someone else. Instead, you're always being camp counsellor. I wonder if that's what motherhood will feel like should I ever end up in spawning mode.

The Christmas decorations are all going up now, which is, let's face it, depressing, but at least they do it tastefully here. Christmas lights always bugged me growing up because it was like (literally) hanging up a big electric sign on your house that said, "I spent $18.95 on this electric sign."

Tonight I've been in the local Internet café, and right now I'm back in the hostel. K is with his posse at a bar in Shoreditch that plays Canadian football on its TV. Now *there's* a smart business decision for some wise pub owner. He must truly lure in the locals with *that*. Sometimes I wonder if I'm actually here in London. Honestly, the best news I had today was an email telling me that you brought Wayne to work yesterday and Shawn spent her smoke break throwing a tennis ball to him. I got jealous.

Weird noises down the hall. Have you ever stayed in a hostel? It's like a crack den without the crack. Never again.

X
B.

PS: I have to add another way that Kyle is driving me nuts. He has a digital camera, and when he shoots something like a bridge or a thousand pigeons, he almost immediately scrolls through his pictures and looks back on what's basically the present moment and treats it like it's the distant past—even if the bridge or the pigeons are still right there.

At the end of the day, I'll scroll through the day's photos with him, and even on the camera's dinky little screen the whole day comes back to me, which is unsurprising, but what *is* surprising are the background details I remember that I might never have remembered otherwise: an Evian truck blowing blue smoke; a woman walking three wiener dogs; a cloud shaped like a muffin. So imagine if you could scroll backwards and look at your whole life the same way. God only knows how many trillions of memories are stored inside us—memories we'll never retrieve simply because we don't have a device that allows us to browse them properly. With your mother, do you think the memories were still locked inside her and she couldn't retrieve them? Or do you think the memories were simply gone? Is anyone's existence only as good as their brain is at any given moment? And if so, what about the soul?

BONUS TREAT: Another brief attempt to address the bread buttering issue is on the next page. B.

The ToasTron Chronicles

Neo-London, 2110

Slice Number Six informed his lieutenant of the entire gory tale behind the marmalade algorithms stolen from Baking Asteroid Teflon 32. Number Six—known simply as "Slice" to his SubLoaf—radiated manly confidence to his squad, who were exhausted from a century of warring with an alliance comprised of Beaten Egg regiments, Vanilla Androids, small factions of Milk and, of course, the French.

"Lieutenant, sir, there's never been an uprising like it. And the Powdered Sugar cluster bombs at the end of the war were an insult to ToasTron and all its fair citizens. The final buttering wasn't war—it was *slaughter*."

. . . Roger, I just don't get sci-fi. How do you guys read this stuff? This buttering ends right here, thank you.

Shawn

Dearest Blair . . .

Boy did the universe hand us Staplers a bone today.

Here's what happened: for once, Roger the alcoholic train wreck decided to actually come in to work on time. He's been on the bottle big time lately, like we don't notice—divorce or some depressing middle-age trip—Pete's been *this* close to firing him. So first Roger went and spent a half-hour reading the paper in the men's room, and then he walked around the store for a while looking more like a homeless person who found a Staples outfit in a Dumpster than a Staples employee. Then he went into the office, scrawled a letter or something, then told us he had to take his dog to the vet (which, okay, you can't really get mad at him about, but it was Dell Day and poor Fahad had to do the brunt of the loading work even though he has the muscle tone of a Jerry's Kid).

So Roger went out to his car, and then he came inside maybe five minutes later and he smelled like . . . the worst sort of . . . *shit* . . . like a decaying fecal poo monster, and he was *covered* in the stuff. I was in the staff room and smelled it before I saw it and said, "Roger, what the hell?" and he said his dog had just shat all over the inside of his car, and so I said, "So, then, don't come back inside here, and jeez, take a shower!" He used the staff phone to call his vet and . . . I mean, Blair, you should have *seen* the phone afterwards—it needed an exorcism. You remember Pigpen from Charlie Brown—how he always had that little vermin cloud following him? Well, that was the phone. Later on, we ended up dousing it with half a bottle of

Windex, which fried its circuits, so now we don't have a staff phone—but I'm getting off topic.

So Roger went driving off in his shit heap (ha!) and I was standing there looking at the phone like it was a six-hundred-pound circus freak with a two-hundred-pound goiter when I noticed that Roger had left something behind on the counter. *What*, I thought, *is this? It* was (get this) a novel Roger has been writing. Can you believe it? Him, boozehound loser, writing a book. And he'd really gone to town on it, using all the products we flog here to make documents look better (acetate cover sheets; oak-grained binding strip; forty-pound cream vellum stock . . .), but it still looked like homework. And what, you might ask, is the book called? Again, you won't believe it: *Glove Pond*. Yes, I can hear you thinking, what the hell is *that?* And you would be correct. At the bottom, on the footer, it reads: "*Glove Pond*, by Roger Thorpe. Currently negotiating representation." Gee, Roger, all of New York must be clamouring for this little Pulitzer contender.

Blair . . . it's the *worst* book ever written. It's about these two university people, a married couple, who do nothing but drink Scotch and shriek at each other, and then a young writer and his wife come over for dinner and they get sucked into the downward failure spiral of fighting and shrieking, and there's a mysterious child who the professors either do or do not have and . . . well, I do have to hand it to Roger, I read through the whole thing as far as he'd written it. But here's the best (and worst) part, Blair: *part of it is set here at Staples.*

Can you bear it?

One of the characters works here—it's basically Roger,

disguised as someone else—and he talks about how much he hates coming to work here (touché to that!), and I have to say, it's weird seeing your everyday reality, stupid and dreamless as it is, turned into a book. Suddenly it's not stupid and dreamless any more, it becomes different—even if it's a book by Roger Thorpe. And an interesting part of it is that he's used our close personal friend, Dawn-of-the-Dead Bethany, and her studly duddly Kyle as models for his characters. (You and I have gone over the Kyle/Bethany thing a million times, and I'll never quite figure out why it happened), but old Roger can't be *too* clueless if he picked up on the World's Weirdest Fling.

Well, whatever.

What happened next is I took Roger's oeuvre over to the copy department and used my coffee break to disassemble the book and make twenty copies. It was a lot of work, and it reminded me of my two years in hell doing nighttime copier shift.

And then the power went out—a seasonal windstorm—always fun because we get to herd out the customers, lock the doors and slack off. Which is exactly what we did, and then we headed into the staff room and read *Glove Pond*.

Did I say it was awful? It's *horrific*. After a few minutes, we all began doing *Glove Pond* impersonations. Kind of like:

> Steve: Gloria, hand me some Scotch.
> Gloria: No, because I'm drinking the Scotch.
> Steve: Let's both drink Scotch, and then we can say witty things to each other.
> Gloria: I hate you.

Steve: I hate you too, you hag.

Gloria: I throw my Scotch in your face.

Steve: I hate you.

Gloria: Do we have more ice cubes?

Steve: I don't think so.

Gloria: Where are our guests?

Steve: Let's drink more Scotch.

After two hours, the power came back on, and we'd actually gotten pretty good at being Steve and Gloria. Around three o'clock, Roger returned to work, and he was a total basket case. He was wearing his old-model Staples shirt from a year and a half ago, before the new ones came out, and his hair had just been washed and gelled, but he looked like a street person with a totally deranged look in his eyes. Simon asked how his dog was, and Roger said he's okay. It ate some of his kid's chocolate (which is like poison to dogs), hence the *merde*ification of Roger's Hyundai.

That was when I heard Tracy shout across the store to Geoff in the copier area, "Storeroom, pass me some Scotch! I need some Scotch!"

Geoff shouted back, "It's my Scotch, you fraud. Pour your own Scotch."

Roger's head perked up like a dog that hears his master's engine approaching from three blocks away.

Jen was up at the till and called out over the PA system, "Gloria, we need a price check on Scotch," to which Geoff PA'ed back, "Not for you, you old battle-axe."

"Aren't we being witty today?"

"You shrill witch."

Of course we were all laughing—it was funny! And Jen and Geoff kept it going, too:

"You failure! You're a failure of a teacher, and you can't hold your liquor."

"And you're a failure as a woman, you Scotch-drinking, unwitty person, you."

(Okay, I'm not getting the dialogue exactly right, but you get the picture.)

So what did Roger do? He turned purple is what he did. Obviously, we were all clustered at the ends of his aisle—the pen aisle—to gauge his reaction, and he went totally apeshit and picked up basket after basket of pens and slammed them down on the floor—tens of thousands of pens, Blair—it looked like blue, red and black hay.

Of course, nobody wanted to go near the guy. Would you? So after he'd completely trashed all the Bics, he leaned over to catch his breath. At this point, he could have pulled out an assault rifle and we wouldn't have been surprised. But what did he do? He looked up and then started walking to the front of the store. The people on that end of the aisle quietly split apart, and Roger went up to one of the tills, stared at the gum rack for maybe fifteen seconds, selected a pack of melon-flavoured Bubblicious, pocketed it, then started walking to the staff door out back. Pete, who'd just then come in from that direction and had caught the tail end of all of this, screamed, "Roger, leave—now!"

And so Roger walked out of the store, surrounded by his invisible poo warp and carrying a pack of stolen gum.

All of us looked at the pens on the floor, and Pete looked at me and said, "Shawn, you're in charge of putting these all back in order. Get to it *now*."

So you can see why I'm pissed at the guy.

Blair, consider yourself lucky to have been fired from this place.

I have to go now.

PS: I checked YouTube and, for whatever reason, your gum theft clip has had over 180,000 viewers.

Bethany

That prick Kyle is out of my life. I can't describe what I'm feeling right now . . . but I'll try. For starters, I want to put six bullets through his heart. No, let's get specific—his ventricles—his aorta—his atrium—his cathedral—his fucking World Trade Center.

It was Sunday and we were in this pub restaurant in Hampstead—we'd decided to splurge because we all got sandwiched-out this week. We were there with Jason and Rafe, the jock buddies, and they were acting all weird with telltale ditch-the-girlfriend-and-let's-toss-a-Frisbee faces. So we ate a lunch of roast pork, turnips and mashed potatoes, and when it came time to leave, we were out on the sidewalk, surrounded by moms and dads and kids in strollers and pigeons and cars zooming by, and Kyle told me that he and the jocks were off to some soccer game or something (I was right on that score), but, more importantly, he said, "Bethany, it's over, and it's not like you didn't see it coming." (Actually, I didn't—I saw other crap, but not this.) And never having been dumped before, I had no experiences to draw from, no set of responses—so I just stood there.

"You don't have to make this harder, Bethany. Jesus, say something."

You know what? It didn't even occur to me to ask him *why* he wanted to break up. He babbled on; I waited for something like reality to return to me.

He said, "I think I've been pretty good to you, Bethany. I've never lied to you or stolen anything from you or purposefully fucked with your head."

I asked him what would happen next. He said his stuff had already been packed at the hostel by Denise.

"Denise?"

"Yes, uh—Denise."

Who, you ask, is Denise? Denise is a ho. He apparently met the ho named Denise in Wimbledon a few nights back. All those trips to watch Canadian football at local pubs were apparently something else.

In any event, Kyle told me he was moving to some place in Shepherd's Bush, a neighbourhood in western London.

"Let me get this straight—you've never lied to me or fucked with my head, but as I stand here a slut named Denise is packing—or has already packed—your stuff and you're moving across London with her?"

"You think I planned for this to happen?"

I froze.

. . . *You think I planned for this to happen?*

How many times in the history of human beings has *that* little gem been tossed about? It was like I was watching some old 16 mm instructional film from the 1980s about adrenaline and "fight-or-flight," and I could actually feel enzymes and hormones coursing through me, and the net result was that I became a statue. So Kyle kissed the statue on the forehead and walked away. "Email me." He walked around the corner of a newsagent shop selling KitKats and sandwiches-fucking-sandwiches.

Huh?

I chased after him, and I could see his shoulders hunching up when he heard my voice, and I could also see the annoyed faces of Rafe and Jason. Kyle nodded at them to leave for a second, like he was some big mob capo. I lost it and demanded an explanation to the effect that you don't drag someone halfway around the planet and leave her kicked in the gut outside a restaurant that serves turnip.

"The thing is, Bethany" (and this is what really *did* kick me in the gut) "you're all about death, and that was interesting for a while, but I'm now back in the land of the living. Lately I've been . . . I've been sensing that you don't quite get the gist of breathing and eating and fucking and sleeping and all the other everyday shit that goes with life. It's as if, to you, being alive is a prank that you're playing on the world. I don't get your joke any more."

I said, "But . . ." (and isn't *that* the saddest little one-word sentence in the language?)

And Kyle said, "Sorry. But I have to go. Goodbye, Bethany. Like I said, I didn't plan for this to happen. And some day you'll be in the same spot. So save your judging for then."

And so here I am now, and I don't know what it is I actually am. Loser? Dupe? Dropped bitch? Sucker cow? Royally-screwed-over loser chick who thought she was such hot stuff? My mother was right. That's what kills me here. My mother, the 3X-married DeeDee monster, was on the money about Kyle, and I'm this ungrateful bitch who didn't see wisdom when it was offered, and now I'm marooned in some weird fake crack den in a middle-class English suburb.

And the only person I have to tell this to is you, Roger. I can't tell DeeDee, not yet. And I don't have any friends. Haven't you noticed that? Shawn from aisles 6 and 7? Hardly. I'd phone you, but I don't know your number, and the operator back home says you're unlisted.

There's this old David Bowie song on the radio right now, "Fame"—"Is it any wonder I reject you first?" Fuck you, Kyle.

I'm going to take the Chunnel to Paris, dammit. I'm going to be a woman who took the train to Paris by herself when her lover dumped her outside some shitty pub restaurant in Hampstead.

This is one of those letters best put in the mail right away before the mood leaves me.

Roger, how the hell can you be unlisted? Who do you think you are, the fucking Beatles?

B.

Bethany

VIA FEDEX

Roger,

I wrote you a letter yesterday that I didn't send and won't be sending. Kyle dropped me, and I'm now by myself on the Eurostar to Paris. My head is in a place it's never been before, and I don't have any instructions to tell me what to do next. I'm going to have to come home soon, but I can already see Mom's gloating face.

We just got out of the Chunnel and now we're doing three hundred miles an hour into Paris. I spent a bomb on a first-class ticket—you'd be surprised at how much I've stashed away since my first job bussing tables at a cheesy Mexican restaurant years ago. The car's empty but for me, and they served a nice meal with heavy steel cutlery that someone else will bus. Once I'm in Paris, I'm going to spend another bomb on a good hotel with hot water and clean sheets, no young people, and a concierge who knows how to fill out French FedEx forms.

Outside the window the sky is that deep blue colour that means true night is ten minutes away. Everything outside the window is old, and I ought to care more, but everything over here is old. I hate the past.

Roger, I don't know how I could have been so clueless.

I remember in elementary school walking home once, and this car ran into a cherry tree and all its petals fell at once. That's me right now.

Bye, Roger.

Write me—but I don't know where I'll be, so there's no

address to give you. Isn't that all of life compressed into a sentence?

B.

DeeDee

Hi, Roger.

Your friends at Staples said you weren't working there any longer—that you'd left to finish your novel. Wow, what guts, Roger! I'm impressed. Not everyone could make such a courageous move for their art. Fortunately, *this time* they gave me your home address so I can leave this thank-you note in your mail slot.

Now, let's talk about the flowers you sent me . . . Thank you! I'll take flowers any way I can get them! I felt like a star when they showed up at the office. I felt like Meg Ryan before the perky thing wore off. Yes, there were some white daisies with blue dye in them, like your grandmother would order—but screw it, I got flowers! And Roger, your letter wasn't at all too depressing. It was honest, and that's nice.

I got another "I'm okay, don't worry" email from Bethany. Again, if there's anything you know that would make me feel better about her European voyage, please tell me. I know it's a weird position for you to be in, and will understand if you simply want to stand back and not be involved in another family's issues.

Bye, Roger.

Thanks again,
DD

PS: Before Bethany and I had our scene and she left, she mentioned that you were taking Claritin for some allergies. She said it was making your dreams feel like real life instead of dreams. I think that's what she said. What a strange thing for a drug to do—make things feel "real"—and yet I had the same experience. Your beautiful flowers made me sneeze, so I nipped out to the drugstore and bought some Claritin and took it. When I got home last night, I went to bed and—*hey ho!*—I dreamed I was in a house at night and tornadoes were approaching. I thought it was nuts, because tornadoes only strike during the day, but Bethany was there, clutching a door sill, saying, "Mom, people only *film* tornadoes during daylight. Of course they happen at night, too, even without the sun shining and illuminating them."

Even in my dreams Bethany is more down to earth than me.

Roger, my paper and pen feel so sad.

Bethany

VIA FEDEX

Roger,

Why aren't you writing me? I'm drunk and overwhelmed and I'm in a bistro not far from the Seine—Left Bank—and I have to tell you what happened to me this afternoon. I was leaving my hotel, feeling spaced out and depressed by the Christmas decorations here—not only because they're Christmas decorations and hence automatically depressing, but because they're so much more beautiful and delicate and, I don't know . . . *devoted* than the cardboard schlock we put up in Staples windows. And I felt stupid and young and not worthy of all the beauty these Frenchies soak in every day. It's killing me, all this beauty. I have this feeling the French have X-ray vision and look at me and know that I live with my mother in a Kleenex box on the other side of the planet, that I can't cook, that I watch too much TV and, when I do, it's never the History Channel.

So there I was, walking along, lost inside this downward loser spiral, when I passed this hotel and a man emerged, dressed like a doctor in *All Things Great and Small*—sage greens and browns and that jacket English people wear when *Hello!* magazine visits their country house—and he was walking with two kids and a woman, and then the blood froze in my veins. It was Johnny Depp, right in front of me. And he was this normal guy with normal kids, and I think Vanessa Paradis was in a crabby mood, but he looked my way, our eyes met, he smiled and winked, and then they all got into a Range Rover and left.

Roger, I was standing on the sidewalk for maybe five minutes, trying to digest what had happened. I put my hand to my cheek and felt all this white makeup I've been wearing forever, and I felt so #$%&ing naive and childish. I ran back to my hotel and went to my room, but then, I'd forgotten my key—#$%&ing Europe—and had to go back downstairs to get it. My face was like a mud pie from tears, and I used the shower—this idiotic brassy thing that's totally hopeless for showering in—and washed away all of the pancake and eyeliner and polonium and all this other crap I've been buried under for five years. And beneath it all is my face, my face that I've never been able to look at for very long. My relationship with the mirror is usually like locking eyes with a stranger on a bus and then looking away. But this time I didn't look away, and there was foolish, naive, pink, blubbery, boring, nothing little me. If I saw me on a bus I'd snicker and say, "Well. At least I'm not her." But I am.

Roger, I feel so stupid, and I'm trying to drink myself into feeling numb, and I've never done that before. I think there's much to be said for feeling numb. Time passes more quickly. You eat less, and because numbness encourages laziness, you do fewer things, good or bad, and the world's probably a better place. Being numb makes you a crime fighter! Is that what happened with you? Selfish me—I write you a letter and talk about nothing but me. How is Zoë? How's Staples? How's the weather? I scour the *International Herald Tribune* every day, and you have no idea how good it makes me feel to know that, back home, the daily high is two degrees Celsius and it's partly cloudy. I can see the parking lot at work: abandoned shopping carts, a thin crust of road salt, SUVs coming and going—how depressing that visions of a parking lot can make me homesick.

For dinner I ordered mussels—*moules marinère*. Have you ever tasted those things? They taste like catshit scraped off a dock. I ate exactly one, then tried to wash the taste away with pastis (that licorice liqueur), but now I can feel the mussel in my stomach breeding, multiplying, expanding, having babies . . . I'm hoping it's not a rough night tonight.

I just looked up at all the tiny yellowy-white lights they've lit for Christmas. They go all the way down the street, some brighter than others, some a different shade of white. Of all things, I'm remembering that astronomy book my mother left in the bathroom to try and lure me into the world of science and nursing. It described the asteroid belt. Most people don't know what the asteroid belt is. It's this gap between Mars and Jupiter where a planet used to be. To be more precise, scientists think there used to be a planet there with a big moon, but they got too closely entangled in each other's orbits and they collided and shattered. How romantic, in a Japanese manga kind of way.

It's so fucking *old* here, Roger, so fucking *old*. The concierge told me they don't allow anything to be built that might prevent them from making Paris look like the seventeenth century if a movie were to be filmed.

I have to stop writing this now. *Garçon!*

Bethany

PS: Don't forget, you can always email me at blackchandelier@gmail.com.

Bethany

VIA FEDEX

Roger,

I ran out of money staying at the swankypants hotel, pretending I was Mademoiselle Fifi. I don't know what I was thinking—I sat there in the hotel, and I could feel the money leaving my body, but I didn't move, and now I'm broke. I went to the airline office here and it turned out I couldn't use my ticket to fly home early because it was some special fare deal, but I *was* able to switch it so I don't have to go back to London to catch the flight. I'm stuck in a hostel again, except this one is in eastern Paris and it makes the hostel in Hampstead look like the Four Seasons. It's full of Russian skinhead hash dealers who listen to nothing but reggae music. I'm convinced they spend their free time, when they're not selling hash, stealing purses from French housewives. I'm afraid to leave my stuff here, so when I go out to get something to eat I take anything remotely valuable with me. I catch a train to Frankfurt tomorrow to fly home on a direct flight. If I don't screw up, I'll get back with one euro in my pocket.

Going outside here is torture—I can barely look at my clothes or wear them. They're so shabby and passé and juvenile. Black clothes look good only when they're brand new or recently dry-cleaned. When I put on my old clothes, I feel so deranged, and I'm convinced people on the street are staring at me like I escaped from a group home. A few weeks ago that would have made me happy. Now I feel like a loser.

But that's not the biggest or weirdest news, which is this: I bumped into Mr. Rant yesterday! Wow, huh? He was in St-Germain-des-Prés looking into a florist's window. He turned around, looked at me and said, "Hey, I need a replacement toner cartridge for an HP LaserJet 1320. Where do I find one?" I was so homesick and lonely that I hugged him. Him being him, he said, "Oh. You look different without your face all whited out. What are you doing in this nightmare of a country?"

I explained my situation to him. His name is Greg. Isn't that old-fashioned? Imagine naming your kid Greg these days. I can see the woman typing the name on the hospital form pausing for a second and looking up at you to make sure you aren't joking.

So anyway, Greg took me for lunch, and if you'd told me two months ago that a lunch with Mr. Rant would be the best thing in my life, I'd have thought you were insane, but there you go. He's here to visit some stainless steel manufacturers. He works for a company in the shipyards back home, and he apparently has to come to Paris every other year for business.

So we went to a bistro where they served generic French food—steak frites, pâté and salade verte. The menu probably hasn't changed in a century. It was so nice to see a familiar face that at first I didn't pay too much attention to his conversation, which was mostly kvetching about the service; the weather; the euro; the hotel mattress; the twenty bucks a day he had to spend to get onto the Internet; the flight over; the pigeons—he went on and on. Then it started to wear me down. I tried pointing out some of the good things here, like the food, and all he could say was, "Trans fat," so I pointed out how well everybody dressed, and he said, "Because they don't have houses to spend money on. They all live in rented apartments and don't own land." I have to tell you, Roger, I began to get *annoyed*. By the time our waiter took away our plates, I snapped. I started shouting at him, and it was awkward because I could tell everybody around us thought we were having a lovers quarrel—*eeyooo!*—and we were, for lack of a better word, "onstage." This, of course, stoked my fires, and I screamed at him something along the lines of, "What the hell is wrong with you? Are you on drugs? Are you on medication or did you stop taking your medication? Why can't you look at the world for even five fucking minutes without trying to trash the place and wreck it for people who maybe might like being here, or who are maybe simply trying to put a good face on being here? Why do you have to wreck everything?"

The poor guy was, possibly for the first time in his life, without words. Then he said, "I didn't realize I was having that effect." He wasn't being snide or anything. I think he genuinely didn't know the effect he has on people.

I said, "Well you *do* have that effect, and I can't stand it. How many friends do you have?"

"What?"

"How many friends do you have?"

"I don't see why that's any of your—"

"It *is* my business. Because you've made me angry. And you don't *have* any friends, *do* you?"

His face said it all.

"I thought so. Doesn't that make you wonder about yourself? Everybody has friends, Greg. Everybody."

"I thought we were simply having lunch here."

"We were. Until you wrecked it with your endless complaining. You're like the psychic equivalent of a wood chipper. Whatever goes in the front comes out the other end in shreds."

Then he delivered a tae kwon do body kick: "You don't have any friends either, do you?"

"I . . . I . . ." I threw some money down on the table—twenty coins' worth of accumulated petty change—and it made a good and rousing noise on the tabletop. "I have lots of friends. And I'm out of here—*Greg*. And by the way, whenever you come into the store, we make fun of you because you're a disaster."

I stormed out before he could make a touché remark—God knows I deserved one—and out on the sidewalk I felt like a total creep. I mean, what if his personality stems from some medical condition and he can't stop himself? Where does your personality end and brain damage begin? And why can't I be normal? Why do I have to be the freak? I don't want to be the freak, but all my life, there I am, out on the edge, the people in my life dropping around me like flies. Broke, wearing pathetic rags in a rectum of a French hostel, eating Mars bars until I catch my plane home. I can't believe I'm coming home, Roger. I feel like such a fail-ure. I was going to become Count Chocula's personal assis-tant. I was going to—

Well, a fat load any of that matters any more. I'll prob-ably get home before this letter reaches you. I have no idea what I'm going to do once I get back, and I don't care. Thanks for being an ear, Roger. I hope your novel has come a long way. It's going to be the worst Christmas ever.

X
Bethany

DeeDee

Hi, Roger!

If I sound cheerful, it's because I am—I got an email from Bethany saying she's returning from Europe. (Didn't say if she's alone or with lover boy, but my mother's intuition tells me she's on her own. Joy to the world!) She got some weird discount Internet ticket, and she flies out of Frankfurt in three days, so I'm preparing the place for her return: I'm renting a big stack of DVDs (the complete Depp oeuvre) and hanging all the Christmas lights (even though Christmas is three weeks away). I bought extra strands to make everything even more festive for her. I also stocked up on all her favourite junk foods. I bet you don't know what her favourite snack is, so I'll tell you: it's saltine crackers with peanut butter on them, BUT she applies room-temperature margarine on top of the peanut butter. Honestly, they look like the coronary tissue from an eighty-nine-year-old woman's heart. But she loves them, and my little girl is coming home, so she can have anything she wants.

Thanks again for last week's flowers, Roger. ~~You didn't need to.~~ It was very important that you did so.

I hope that you and your ex and your daughter and whoever else have a good Christmas this year. Around now, I'm normally a mess, but this year is different—I feel like I'm pregnant and due in three days.

Merry Christmas,
DD

Roger, are you in your apartment but not answering the door? I could swear I heard someone move in there. Don't worry. You probably aren't dressed and shaved. I wouldn't answer the door either. But in the spirit of *Glove Pond*, I'm leaving you a selection of food: a box of pancake mix (no weevils), a dozen eggs, marmalade, butter and a loaf of bread you can use to make lots of toast.

DD

Staples

As you may have heard, Bethany is now back with us, filling in part-time during the holiday season. If any of you need time off before December 24 to help "Santa's Merry Elves" in your own life, we can work with Bethany to arrange a shift change.

Please note that the blank-CD bin at the end of Aisle 12-South has been temporarily moved to allow for retiling.

Fahad

. . . .

PS: Don't forget this year's "Margaritas 'n' Madness" (!!!) on December 22, at 9:00. Fran has rented a table for twenty at the Keg & Cleaver, and if you could give her a five-dollar deposit, that would be great.

. . . .

Bethany

Yes, I'm back at Staples, and there's no need for further comment. Pete was very kind to give me part-time work, especially after last month's hasty vanishing act. But after Europe and all its beauty, it's hard to handle the store's lighting and all the boring products we sell. It feels like we're working inside a photocopier. And the way people dress compared to in Europe? Here we all look like newsies in a Broadway play.

Roger, I'm sorry you got fired. You were the only part of Staples I was looking forward to. And everyone was all too eager to tell me the saga of *Glove Pond*. I am so sorry they did that to you. It physically hurt me when they told me what they'd done, and I had to ask them to stop. They're horrible, nasty little people, but I knew that already, so I can't claim to be surprised. They're pretty much indicative of the world at large. I come in and do my job and don't talk to people. I'm trying to rack up the hours and rebuild some kind of savings, and that's as far as my ambition goes. But I've been rereading *Glove Pond* and love it more than ever, and I hope you're going to finish it. You have to—you can't leave me in the lurch!

Another huge shock to me coming back here was I found a pile of my FedEx'ed letters to you that you'd never received. Shawn asked me why I'd be sending you packages from Europe, so on the spot I made up a lie about doing genealogical research for you. Her curiosity ended there. I guess you didn't know about Kyle and me splitting up. Or Paris. Or Greg. I've attached the unopened FedEx envelopes here. You may as well read about my emotional car crash in proper sequence. I don't want to go into it here.

On the plus side, if you saw me, Roger, you'd see a new, super-healthy Bethany. Mom bought me a Fitness World gym membership, and I go there twice a day. All I eat these days is fresh vegetables, lean meat and gum, but I'm much more clever about stealing it now that the Internet has turned gum thievery into destination viewing. I've washed off my makeup and am trying to go for a girl-next-door look. Maybe even a jock look. Maybe even a mountain climber look, with all those clips and fasteners and nylon fabrics and Velcro flaps everywhere. Europe walloped the Goth right out of me.

It's been a long week, Roger. Things with Mom haven't been so hot, and I'm tired from the gym and the jet lag and all the shifts I'm doing. Everyone knows I messed up majorly. Instead of getting, "How was your trip!" I'm getting, "Oh, uh, lookin' good, Bethany," followed by averted eyes. I suppose they'll forget this episode soon enough— the gossip must be fading, though who knows what Kyle's been emailing them. God, has it been only four weeks? It feels like a year. It feels like—or rather, *I* feel like a different person. So Europe worked its magic in the end, but . . . this isn't the person I wanted to become.

Gotta go, Roger. Jamie's picking up a Maltipoo puppy for her father's surprise Xmas present and I'm covering her shift. I've never worked Aisle 9-South before. Life is such a rich buffet of experiences.

How are you, Roger? Tell me. I'm listening.

B.

DeeDee

Roger,

I'm bringing you more *Glove Pond* theme food: Triscuits, orange cheddar cheese and (instead of Scotch) a $20 bottle of Sonoma Valley chardonnay. I'm assuming you won't answer the door when I ring, so I'll put it in this box outside your door and hope the raccoons don't steal it. There's no trace of the last care package I left you, so I think it'll be okay.

Bethany told me what happened at the store. What a disgraceful way to treat such an amazing piece of work—*Glove Pond* is marvellous, Roger, and you shouldn't pay attention to a bunch of ignorant fetuses. They're jealous. I mean, in an era when nobody achieves anything, *you* started a novel— that's something huge. The only thing any of those twerps have ever started is lifelong credit card debt. Keep on writing. I'll be honoured to be your test audience if you let me.

Now—about Bethany—Roger, I'll go ~~insane~~ ~~mental~~ ~~bonkers~~ nuts if I don't vent about Little Miss Fresh Air and Exercise. What is *wrong* with her? She doesn't eat except bits of raw fish she removes from the rice part of sushi. And grapefruit juice. She sleeps with her windows wide open, and her room is like a deep freeze. She gave away all of her Goth clothing. I went to the drop box after she dumped it and retrieved it all. She doesn't know, but she'll thank me for it one day— Goth may look grim, but the stuff is expensive, let me tell you.

The biggest and strangest thing is that she won't argue with me any more. If I say something to provoke her, like "Use a coaster for your coffee cup," she apologizes—I mean grovelling apologizing. She didn't even mock the Christmas lights and call me middle class or a religious victim. She said they were pretty and hugged me. I feel like she's been body-snatched, and I don't have a clue who this new person is. The hardest thing was when I made popcorn for a late-night movie and I was wearing my aqua sweatpants and looked like a big fat Crisco-bitch. When I came into the TV area, I was hoping she'd make a wisecrack, but instead she said, "Mom, I think it's great that you're okay with the way you are." God, young people can be patronizing, but I don't think she meant it that way. I think maybe she *is* okay with the fact that I'm a disaster, which scares the shit out of me because I *must* be one, then. Cripes.

So I couldn't eat the popcorn, and during commercials I went into the bathroom to look at myself in the mirror, trying to pretend I was someone else, and I was horrified. Roger, tell me that I was once beautiful. I need that. I know I'm fishing here, big time, but there's so little gas left in my tank. I'm running on fumes.

And what do I do with Sunshine Girl—any recommendations? Get her to a therapist? She reminds me of a girl in high school going through a nun phase. I ought to be happy that Bethany's trying to slim down, but she's doing it for reasons I don't know, and a mother's instinct tells me they're the wrong reasons.

There.

I've gotten that out of my system.

Roger, if you could work some more on *Glove Pond*, it would really inspire and motivate Bethany. Is there any chance?

X
DD

Roger

DeeDee . . .

When Brendan was killed on his bike (Capilano Road at Canyon Boulevard; Sunday afternoon; no drunk driver, merely an accident), I knew life was over and something else was beginning. I'd still be alive and all, but it couldn't be called a "life." Joan knew it too. We never discussed it, but since that afternoon we've never been able to look each other in the eyes, not really. Joan went the therapy route, and she likes to think she can look me in the eye, but it's a fake look and she knows I know. Zoë was too young to remember any of it.

I quit my job selling off-season ski resort time-shares because I couldn't stand the sensation of everybody looking at me at my desk and whispering about what happened to Brendan. I stopped seeing everybody who knew me before Brendan's death. It's why I joined that goddam dinner theatre company, because it was a clean slate. I can't even act. I was just browsing through the *Weekend Shopper*, and I recognized it as a potential haven, full of strangers, and I could maybe get lost in it. It wasn't hard. As in any milieu, there's always an extra slot in the theatre world for somebody who's punctual and who doesn't gossip, so I was opening and closing curtains and stacking chairs right away.

Enter sex. Enter Diana Tigg. Enter the raging, self-absorbed hose-monster—the diseased harridan who played the lead in *Same Time, Next Year*. (*Thinking of dinner and a play? Think of the North Shore Players and the Keg & Cleaver's limited-time-only mid-week two-for-one*

Bard's Buffet. Bravo!) I don't expect any sympathy regarding the woman, because I don't deserve any—I deserve heaps of scorn. I briefly fell for an *actress*, a remorseless pulsing quasar of infinite joy-sucking neediness and petty vengeance.

Like any so-so actress, *la Tigg* was more interesting in real life than onstage. There's the old truism about how we're all poor actors strutting about a stage and then we die—well, *I* don't believe it. Next time you're out in public, watch every ordinary person perform even the tiniest of gestures with total grace and fluency—picking up their dry cleaning, say, as they mumble about the day's weather with the Korean mama-san who runs the place, all the while plucking coins from the recesses of their wallets and purses. Masterful. But if you'd beforehand given any one of these people the same lines in a script? They'd flub it. They'd botch real life.

That's where Diana comes in. The woman was unable to be natural. She really treated everyday life as theatre, but instead of scripts she had only fragments she'd borrowed from other plays—words and mannerisms she'd copied from TV soap operas. She certainly couldn't write her own material, and she had the God-given absence of any ability to analyze the effect she had on people. She never knew when to slow down or speed up or shut up, but before I figured out her act, we met at her place and things went . . . the way they did. Within forty-eight hours, she was leaving guess what kind of messages on my home answering machine, which Joan immediately intercepted, and out the door I went. And the worst part of it was that, in the end, Diana had made it with me only as pity sex—a ticket girl who used to temp at my ski office had blabbed my story about Brendan to the troupe.

So long to the remains of my old existence . . . and hello to a basement suite, as well as to Staples, a workplace so incredibly anonymous and depersonalized that I revelled in its sterility—the total absence of community. And I had Mr. Vodka to help me.

Until I met Bethany I was about as human as a box of discounted tax software. When Bethany accidentally started reading my stuff, suddenly I felt as if . . . maybe creativity could save me, maybe I could invent a more desirable world. And maybe I could salvage something from all the crap and loss and pain and—and maybe I could become rich! And maybe . . . well, all the typical wannabe's maybes.

The last few weeks haven't been my finest hour. I have Wayne and, once in a blue moon, Zoë.

I'll try to work on *Glove Pond*. To have true readers on my side makes all the difference. I couldn't do it on my own. Bear with me. Thanks for the food. It all gets eaten.

Roger

PS: By the way, Diana certainly never visited me at Staples. If you ever want to remove an actor from your life, simply tell them they can't act. Poof! They'll be gone, trust me.

It felt like a month had passed since Kyle and Brittany had arrived for dinner at the charming and gracious home of Steve and Gloria. The young couple no longer felt like the people they were when they arrived.

"What college does Kendall go to?" Brittany asked.

"Harvard," said Steve.

Gloria turned and almost spat at him. "I wanted him to go to Yale."

"If you like Yale so much, Gloria, then tell me, what city is Yale located in?"

Gloria froze. "That's dirty pool. Nobody knows what city Yale's located in. It's its own place. It doesn't need a city."

"All you had to say was New Haven."

"I *knew* that. Not telling you the name of the city was my way of telling you how important I think Yale is."

A gleam came to Steve's eyes. "Out of curiosity, Gloria, do you know the name of the city where Harvard is located?"

"Don't be silly."

"Where, then?"

"Harvard is Harvard." She paused. "Why, we visited Kendall there a few weeks ago. Don't you remember?

We dropped off snacks and a box full of domestic comforts."

The word "Kendall" brought Steve back to what passed for reality in the dining room. "Of course we did." Steve looked at Kyle and Brittany. "Kendall is an excellent student. We visit him regularly."

Kyle asked, "Are you sure you don't have *any* photos of Kendall?—Snapshots? JPEGs? Polaroids? High school yearbooks?"

"No," said Steve.

"Really?"

"None."

"They're all out being cleaned," said Gloria.

"Oh come *on*," said Kyle. "You have to have photos somewhere."

"No," Steve said. "It's the latest thing—sending your photos out to be cleaned. Not only do they come back looking like new, but they're also arranged neatly in stylish new photo binders."

"That's ridiculous," said Kyle. "There has to be *something* here somewhere."

"Say," said Steve. "You know what we *do* have is a large selection of Kendall's toys. We can show you those."

"Why would I want to look at toys?" Kyle asked.

"Don't move," said Gloria. "I'll be right back."

"Really, Gloria—you don't have to . . ."

But Gloria scurried away to the basement, and Steve was hearty. "Kendall was a good child. He loved his toys. Scotch?"

Kyle looked at Brittany, who appeared far away. "Brit?"

"Oh—sorry. I was looking at the clock over there."

"Wretched things, clocks," said Steve. "Give me an hourglass or a sundial any day of the week."

From the basement came rattling noises, and Steve poured more Scotch for Kyle. He then looked at Brittany. "So tell me, how is life different with makeup covering your face all the time?"

"This?" Brittany put her hand to her cheek, massaged the tissue and looked at the resulting kabuki ovals on her fingertips. "I think I'm over makeup now," she said. "It protected me for a while, but it's like a magic spell. Once you lose faith in it, it's merely more junk in life."

Kyle gulped his Scotch.

Silence made Gloria's rattling in the basement more menacing. Steve said, "What's a JPEG? You used that word a few minutes back."

"A JPEG?" said Kyle. "It's an image you send around on computers."

"Why is it called a JPEG?"

Brittany said, "It's an acronym for Joint Photographics Experts Group."

"*This*pegs, *that*pegs—why can't people be happy with a sepia-tinted daguerreotype? Ah, look, here comes Gloria with a comprehensive selection of young Kendall's toys."

From the basement's portal—a door over towards the kitchen—came a dreadful drumming sound that became higher in pitch as Gloria neared the dining room. With small beads of sweat percolating through the pancaked cosmetic stratas atop her brow, she staggered through the doorway and dumped a pile of

weatherworn plastic animals, pedal carts and miscella-
neous outdoor toys. "There!" she said. "Kendall's toys.
He exists."

Glove Pond: Brittany

Brittany decided not to tell Kyle about the origins of Kendall's toys. Why bother? Steve and Gloria were eccentric, to say the least, but *nuts*? Maybe not. She certainly wondered how a child belonging to this couple might have turned out. The absence of Kendall photos was suspicious, but if Kendall had half a brain, he probably would have fled the nest at the first possible moment. Maybe he took his photos with him.

This makeup is annoying me.

Brittany remembered applying it up in Gloria's pink boudoir, remembered how strangely liberated she felt once she put it on—the way it allowed her to briefly reincarnate as someone new who wasn't so wrapped up in the world and its problems. But she was tiring of it now. It was a brief phase in her life; she already felt herself entering a new one.

Meanwhile, Steve and Gloria were going through "Kendall's" toys, one by one.

"Ah," said Steve. "Kendall's novelty scooter, emblazoned with a cartoon fish to help him roar out into the world." The fish was from Walt Disney's *Finding Nemo*, which would have made Kendall at most, twelve.

"Isn't this precious!" said Gloria, holding a thrashed yellow loop. "Kendall's favourite hula hoop!"

"He loved that hula hoop, didn't he?" said Steve with the zest of a teenager who's learned a new swear word. "Newfangled things. Took us all by surprise, they did." Steve looked at Brittany and Kyle, their brains rigorously calculating an estimate of Steve's age. "I'm kidding," Steve said. "I'm not *that* old."

Gloria pounced on a small Fisher-Price choo-choo train, stripped of its primary colours by too many winters and too much sun, its plastic palpably disintegrating. "Watch what happens when I run this along the floor," she said, falling to her knees on the Persian rug, "It makes this darling little toot-toot noise." The little choo-choo train's beeps made it sound like it had emphysema. Gloria and Steve beamed like proud parents.

Extreme empty nest syndrome? Alcoholic psychosis?

Steve sat down on the floor as well, spilling a drop of Scotch on his pants. "Look at this!" he said. "A plastic puppy!"

"I'll be back in a moment," Brittany said. She fled to the guest bathroom, a dusty little place with one functioning light bulb. Kyle's first chapter was lying atop the cistern. She ran the water. The hot wasn't on, so she rinsed her face with cold water, then looked around for soap, finding only the vintage soap shards.

She scrubbed at her face and watched the residue vanish down the drain like milk until finally the water was clear. There were no guest towels. Under her breath she said, "No disrespect, Kyle," and used his first chapter to sluice the water from her skin.

Shaking her hands to hasten drying, she left the bathroom, grabbed her coat and went out the front door.

"I'm just getting a bit of fresh air, guys. Back in a short while."

She stepped out into what had become a night so cold it made the stars vibrate.

Bethany

Hey Roger,

Glove Pond is back—thank you. And it was genius that you FedEx'ed it to me from your place. I think Mom's boss truly is going to shit nickels when he gets the FedEx bill, but so what. As Gloria says, art must come first. And it's funny to think that, during the night, it had to fly all the way to Kentucky or wherever first before coming back here.

I lost six pounds this week. Not bad. All these shifts and my gym membership are paying off royally, and I *don't* think it's bad or scary for me to take an interest in my body. I can become strong. I *can*. I can become something lean and cat-like, someone whom the world will look at and go, *Whoa, there's one ass-kicking wench*.

I couldn't sleep last night and there was this old Stephen King movie on channel 62 in which almost everybody on a jumbo jet headed to Boston vanishes in midflight except for these six people who were asleep. So these six people wake up, and in the seats where all of the vanished passengers had been sitting was the clothing and shoes they'd been wearing. I suppose the director wanted us to think, *Ooh, their bodies left, but* only *their bodies. Everything that wasn't a part of their bodies stayed behind!* But this is total crap. What *would* be left behind if everything that was you vanished? The only thing that's truly *you* is cells containing your DNA. So that means everything that isn't a DNA-bearing cell would be left behind on the 747. So yes, there'd be clothing and shoes, but there'd also be dental fillings, breast implants, hair weaves, false eyelashes, porcelain veneers, makeup, contact lenses, nail polish, artificial hips, donated kidneys, artificial hearts, pacemakers, cologne, heart stents—and if you think about it further, all the non-DNA stuff from inside the body: undigested food, bacteria, viruses, prions, snot, earwax, piss and drugs. And then the last thing of all would be the water that keeps everything going—gallons of water, because water doesn't have any DNA in it. Saliva would be left behind too, except for shed skin cells from within the mouth. BTW, that's how they nailed the Unabomber: from shed mouth cells in the saliva he'd used to moisten the flaps of his bomb-loaded envelopes. I think even eggs and sperm would be left behind, because aren't they only half of a DNA strand searching for another half?

So back up in the jumbo jet there'd be 250 seats containing ugly puddles of soggy crap where there used to be people. Imagine the smell.

Let's go further. Forget what got left behind in the plane's seats—what would it be, then, that was actually taken *away* in this movie's rapture event-thingy? Some weird, completely dehydrated beef jerky thing? Maybe not even that—we'd be like pantyhose.

Wait—I'm not sure if bones count.

Let me google it.

Five minutes later: Know what? Bones don't contain DNA, but marrow *does*, thus skeletons minus the marrow would be left behind inside the 747. Hair, it turns out, contains no DNA either—only the roots—so hair would be left behind as well. And don't forget teeth, minus the pulp inside them. In fact, what we think of as our bodies is only partially "us." We're made of filler. We're hot dogs, Roger. DNA is basically this containment system required to hold all of the goop we flatter ourselves into thinking is so holy.

But . . . it turns out I was wrong about the sperm thing. Sperm contains fifty times as much DNA as blood does. It's a forensic bonanza. Weird, huh? But here's something I could never figure out. I remember looking at my high school yearbook and thinking it was strange that there were an equal number of girls and boys. Let's face it—there ought to be one guy for every hundred women. One trillion sperm for every egg? What was nature thinking? It's always struck me as nutty. I remember watching documentaries about WWII, how in Germany in 1946 there were two women for every man, and even at the age of six, I thought, *Yeah, that sounds far more realistic.*

Time to change the subject.

Random fact: If you chug a gallon of whole milk, within one hour you'll puke yourself clean.

Interruption . . .

Yves from the printing counter was wondering if I've seen his cellphone. He's one of those guys who buys all of his Christmas presents at a 7-Eleven on Christmas Eve— his family members get copies of *Vanity Fair* wrapped in Reynolds Wrap.

Yeah, Bethany, like you're totally into Christmas or something.

Thank you, interior monologue. You are correct. I am being a hypocrite.

But what was the universe thinking when it came up with Christmas? *Hey, let's wreck six weeks of the year with guilt and loneliness and unnecessary cheesy crap! And then let's invent office superstores where they can take everyday stuff like pens and glossy printer paper and commit an emotional travesty by suggesting these items as gift ideas for loved ones!*

I think Christmas is about that point where we as humans split off from the rest of the universe and became prisoners of ourselves instead of being unselfconscious and free like the animals and birds. Yes, we received cars and jets and Hollywood motion pictures, but we also got saddled with calendars and time—the fact that there's either too much of it, or too little. And we also got saddled with the knowledge that we can either make use of time doing worthwhile things or fritter it away watching *Partridge Family* marathons on satellite TV stations while drinking one of the countless new energy drinks that have appeared on the market overnight. I like Red Bull because it tastes like penicillin. Sick, huh?

Coffee break over. I have to go tidy up the bargain CD bin.

Joy to the world.

I'm going to show my mother the new chapters. She's your biggest fan.

And you still haven't told me how you are.

B.

PS: It's five minutes later and I had to come back in and add this. I think Christmas celebrates the moment in our history as a species when we stopped being prey and began making weapons and traps and turned into predators— like those apes at the start of *2001*. There's never been another species that's done that. We *are* unique. We changed modes.

Glove Pond: Kyle

The doorbell rang.

Kyle wondered if he might learn why his hosts had taken five minutes to answer the bell when he and Brittany arrived. No such information was forthcoming. Gloria put down Kendall's plastic choo-choo train, patted her hair and went to answer it, revealing a tall, thin, generically aristocratic white-haired man in a tweed coat frayed at the elbows, his ears pink from the cold. She was thrilled. "Why—it's acclaimed theatrical director and curmudgeonly-yet-sophisticated man about town, Leonard Van Cleef! Hello, Leonard. Welcome to my charming and gracious home!"

"Yeah. Hiya, Gloria." Leonard rubbed his hands and walked in.

Steve was still on the floor, idly playing with Kendall's *Finding Nemo* plastic scooter. "Hello, Leonard."

"Hello, Steve."

"Can I get you a drink?"

"Scotch, if you have any."

"Right."

Kyle sensed no warmth between the two men. Gloria, meanwhile, stood beside a chair, practising alluring come-hither poses. "What brings you out tonight?"

"I thought we might discuss the play a little bit."

"Really?" Gloria's eyes saucered. "Of course we can discuss the play. We *must*. Art must always come first."

Kyle coughed.

"Oh, I'm sorry," said Gloria. "Please let me introduce you to tonight's dinner guest—" Gloria's pose reminded Kyle of nineteenth-century kill shots of British lords brandishing muskets above gargantuan slain leopards. "This is acclaimed and rich young novelist Kyle Falconcrest. Kyle and his wife are here for dinner tonight. Nothing fussy—Chinese takeout. That's the way we like it here at our house: friendly, informal, casual, and yet charming and gracious at the same time."

"Jeez." Leonard looked at Kyle. "You a relative or something?"

"Nope."

"Small mercies. These two take the cake."

Steve handed Leonard his Scotch. Leonard swished it around in its tumbler, then surveyed the room around him. "Nice digs. Been living here long?"

"Since my first novel came out."

Gloria burst in, "It garnered good reviews but didn't sell much."

"Huh."

Steve sipped his drink and Gloria said, "Kyle's last book sold ten million copies."

Leonard looked at Kyle as though Kyle had sprouted antlers. "Really?"

"Uh—yes."

"Would have to have been something pretty broad

to sell that much. What was it—a batch of kittens secretly takes over a weight-loss clinic? And then the kittens turn a ragtag bunch of losers into skinny people with rich sex lives and unconditional love from their family members?"

"That actually *would* be a big seller," said Kyle.

"What's a weight-loss clinic?" asked Steve.

"Oh, *Steve*," chided Gloria. "Everyone knows what a weight-loss clinic is. People go to them all the time. They're very popular. You use their scientifically designed programs to lose weight while Hollywood celebrities and members of the British royal family support you through posters and brochures, urging you onward with little homilies and bromides. Some of these centres also have tanning salons."

"How do you know so much about this?"

"Oh, *Steve*. Steve, Steve, Steve, Steve, *Steve*." Gloria gave her husband a wise, ageless smile, then looked at Leonard as if to apologize for Steve's inability to keep pace with the times. "None of his novels ever sold very well, you know."

"Wow," said Leonard. "You people *do* take the cake."

Kyle looked at Leonard. "They really do. They're like a John Cheever novel. Except it's set in hell. Check this place out—it's like time stopped ten minutes before they cancelled the Apollo space program."

"You've been snooping?" asked Steve.

"Browsing. Snooping would kick up too much dust." He turned to Leonard. "The whole place is coated in dryer lint."

Three streets away, a truck changed gears. A passing helicopter bunted at the night air.

"Right then," said Leonard. "Enough for witty banter and formalities. I've come here to talk shop. I have news."

DeeDee

Roger,

I'm worried sick about Bethany. She's truly and totally not herself any more. To be honest, she's . . . scary. She washed the dishes last night without being nagged, and then I went into the living room and she was sitting in a chair, not reading or doing anything else, **just sitting in a chair**—which sounds innocent and all, but it's *spooky*. It was like a sci-fi movie where a body-snatched human being is sitting motionless while the invading alien incubates within. And the window was wide open. She thinks that if she stays cold her body will burn more calories and she'll get thin.

Why does she suddenly care what she looks like? She obviously did during her Goth years, but that was an act of rebellion, whereas this new exercise and dieting craze feels like the worst sort of conformity. Nothing would make me happier today than to see Bethany walk into the living room eating a bowl of Creamsicle ice cream while lecturing me about my directionless lifestyle and wearing a black Cure tank top with her eyes blacked out like Alice Cooper. Alice Cooper isn't strictly Goth, I know that, but you know what I mean. Where did the real Bethany go? What happened in Europe? She won't discuss it. Okay, she got dumped, but if I try to use the I've-been-there tone of voice, she gives me the yes-but-you-always-get-dumped-in-the-end tone of voice. *So who are you to offer advice?*

Oh, her little broken heart! Now I'm crying, Roger. Imagine Bethany's tiny little broken black heart, lying on some cobbled London thoroughfare like a piece of litter!

I can barely remember my first heartbreak. I used to fall in love so easily, falling out of love always emerged as an inevitable end product. Sometimes I remember being happy with someone, and then panicking and pretty much choosing to fall out of love just so I wouldn't get dumped. Only a young person could do something that stupid. It's only now that I'm past the point when I'll ever again be loved that I know how sacred the whole process is. Ain't life a kick in the teeth?

If you can think of *some* way to make her be herself again, please be a friend to me—and to her—and share the idea.

DD

PS: It's funny how often I think about Steve and Gloria.

Roger

Bethany . . .

The last two weeks of the year are the worst two weeks of the year. Who the hell invented December? *Curse you, Pope Gregory*. It's a disaster of a month, a complete waste of thirty-one days. And it's not like early January's much better.

I didn't know about Kyle—I hope it's not too weird, me mentioning him by name. He's a creep, and he's out of your picture. At least you saw his true colours quickly, albeit thousands of miles from home. Did you get anything out of Europe besides a theatrical backdrop for a bad personal situation? There's a part of me that's actually jealous that you got to go to Europe in love, and that you got to feel something intensely. I'm showing my age, but send me a postcard when you're in your forties and see if you don't agree.

The important thing is to not obsess on the dark stuff—I can imagine you saying, "Gee, Roger, thanks for the sage advice." But it remains good advice. In twenty years you'll remember the good and the bad more equally. And you *will* get over this. That's the hardest thing of all to believe, that the hurt will dampen and shrink.

More advice: Don't give a rat's ass what your dim-wit co-workers think of any of this. All they care about is which ring tone they should select for their cellphones. They're inconsequential.

And it's good that you're getting into physical activity; you're making me ashamed of my slug lifestyle. Yesterday I went to the corner store for orange juice then to a coffee shop to steal a morning paper. Calories expended: thirty-seven. I'm a coronary statistic in waiting.

You've been asking how I'm feeling. The answer is not too great, but it's best not to go into it. I'm actually glad to be out of Staples, and I had a great afternoon with Zoë last week skating on the lake up Grouse Mountain. It was very *Charlie Brown Christmas*. What's making me feel marooned inside my own life is not knowing what I'm going to do next, but I think that happens to folks my age even when their lives are still on the rails. I hang in there.

So, my friend, go easy on yourself. You have people in your life who care about you. Not everyone can say that. I spoke with Steve and Gloria this afternoon, and they both recommend that you keep a diary—you'll treasure it one day.

Roger

Glove Pond: Brittany

Brittany's night walk was lit by a scrim of stars and serenaded by muffled suburban noises—a barking dog; a teenager burning out in a blue Honda; transformers humming atop telephone poles. She couldn't remember the last time she'd walked for the sake of walking. She always had to have a reason for walking; some productivity had to be involved: endless brains in need of surgery, galas in need of overachieving attendees. How novel it was merely to roam! To breathe! To (should she want to) sing!

Tonight was the first night in which living things were starting to freeze. She recalled, a few months back, walking across the neurosurgery wing's well-manicured lawn—the end of August?—and she remembered the sensation that her lungs and the air outside were the same temperature. So was the grass. So were the robins darting about the grass and the cicadas chirping in the shrubs. All of these living creatures mingling and coexisting and sharing the world. And then Brittany thought of her own DNA and the DNA of all the creatures surrounding her—quintillions of cells, all of them loaded with DNA, and all of that spiral DNA rotating as mechanically and passionlessly as a car's odometer.

Suddenly, she felt surrounded by billions of little odometers, a universe of churning and grinding and drilling and digging. She felt like her body was turning inside out. She felt her body foaming from within like cumulus clouds. She felt odometers grinding away inside her teeth and bones and flesh.

And now, walking through Steve and Gloria's suburb, she felt life shutting down around her, all of the little odometers slowing down from the cold, yet she was so vibrantly warm and alive—so different from the rest of the world. She felt there was a message she was supposed to be receiving: instructions, clues. And all she could think to do was to continue walking through the world, waiting for whatever it was that was supposed to happen next.

Brittany thought of Steve and she thought of Gloria. She remembered the way Gloria had been massaging her spleen all night. *Dear God—Gloria has spleen cancer.* The diagnosis came to her like that.

She thought some more about Gloria. *Gloria has Alzheimer's.* That's *why she can't remember her lines.*

And then Brittany thought about herself, and suddenly it came to her: *I'm no longer a child. It happened to me when I wasn't looking.*

To: Blair
From: Shawn Paxton
Time: Three hours ago

Blair, you won't believe what happened today amid the Christmas craziness here at the store. (Once again, consider yourself lucky for being canned from this hovel.) I told you that Cruella De Vil came home with her tail between her legs after her big trip to Europe with StudBoy? Well, she got royally dumped (as if it was ever going to last) and then she came back here part-time, which is okay because we all need shift replacements, but she's like a ghost of what she used to be and it's spooky having her around. Like she wasn't already spooky enough, but she's lost all the Goth crap she used to wear and she's trying to be all healthy, which is such a laugh because she's, like, a blimp, and she wears terry socks with the nubbly side on the outside. Clueless.

So it's late afternoon and Cruella is out back, coloursorting file folders. Then, after six weeks away, StudBoy enters the store, and he's with this totally foxy, hot UK bitch. And so everybody's happy to see Kyle again, and we all blow off our customers to go talk to him, and Miss England opens her mouth and she sounds like a Cockney chainsaw, which is a riot, and then everybody has the same thought at the same time, which is, *Can't wait to see Cruella's face when she sees her.* And then Eliza Doolittle says, "So, where's Whatshername?" and with perfect timing Cruella strolls down Aisle 3-South and sees everybody standing there. Then foxy bitch's face collapses and you can tell she's suddenly pissed at StudBoy. She storms out of the place and into the parking lot, where it's dumping rain, and StudBoy follows her, and the moment they get outside, someone's grandma in a Cadillac plows right into the back of the FedEx van, but the ho and StudBoy don't even blink. She's shouting words to the effect of, "You dated *her*? You put me and *her* in the same league?"

Blair, let me tell you, it is truly fun to watch people have a shit fit in the rain beside a car crash. It's like a really good drug that makes time fly. Everybody in the store—staff and customers alike—came out to view the fun, but if anybody was smart, they should have been inside the store, shoplifting the brains out of the place. You could have walked out with an office chair stashed under your jacket and we wouldn't have noticed.

Anyway, I have to say I felt a little bit sorry for poor Cruella, but she looked like the drama didn't bug her, and within a minute she was back to sorting folders again. It's hard to imagine her having much of an inner life. The Goth thing was total bullshit.

Break time is over.

Are you coming to the lame-o company party this year?

S

Bethany

Roger, I have to write to you or I'll go nuts. ~~The last few days it feels like real life and my dream life are joining together and I can't tell which is which. Out of nowhere, I see pictures of burning houses and people being thrown violently around rooms. Cars falling from the sky and crushing pizza parlours. Drowned teenagers walking out of the sea. Homeless men in parking lots having fist fights and battling for control of stolen souls. A tornado will come down from above and suck away both the earth and the sky. Crazy shit. And the more I try not to think about it, the more it happens. So then I try to think of the opposite of these scary pictures. I try to think of a perfect city where it's always bright and where people don't die—a place where you can have turkey dinners or read good books any time you want and where there's always new space on your arm for a cool tattoo—but those pictures never click, and instead I wonder if I'm awake or asleep, and whether I should stab myself with a fork to see which one it is: reality or dream.~~

Kyle is back in town, and he brought his ho to the store—and if I ever wondered what it feels like to be a bacterium under a microscope's lens, I now know. It was so stupid and cruel of him. So cruel. What was he hoping to gain by it? And all eyes were on me, just waiting, waiting, waiting for me to create a scene, but I wouldn't give them that satisfaction.

Roger, this past month has been so hard, and your being fired was almost too much for me. ~~In my head there was always the fact~~ Before that, when life was horrible

I could always tell myself, *Yes, well at least Roger's in this with me.*

Oh God, I'm sitting here and my inner voice won't shut up. Do you ever get that? All you crave is silence, but instead you sit there and, against your wishes, nag yourself at full volume? *Money! Loneliness! Failure! Sex! Body! Enemies! Regrets!*

And everybody's doing the same thing—friends, family, that lady at the gas station till, your favourite movie star—everyone's skull is buzzing with *me, me, me, me, me,* and nobody knows how to shut it off. We're a planet of selfish me-robots. I hate it. I try to turn it off. The only thing that works is if I try to imagine what it's like to be inside someone else's head, try to imagine what *their* inner nagging is. It cools my brain. That's what I liked about *Glove Pond*, Roger, that you were being someone else. And it's what I liked a few months back, when you pretended you were me. I suppose it's what makes Greg so funny, that he's thinking the same crazy, self-centred bullshit as everybody else, but with him we get to hear it with the volume turned up.

God, I'm so *sick* of myself.

Oh, Roger, I truly wish I'd had religion growing up, because believing in something might shut off my inner voice—and maybe also so that I could feel like I shared something with my family, a common vision. All I got from my family is death, divorce and desertion. Please come up with ideas to share with Zoë. She'll probably hate you until she's twenty-one, but after that she'll thank you forever. You're so lucky to have the chance to not screw somebody up.

You know, I was at the gym an hour ago, using a bench press, and my head was upside down and I was looking out the windows and there were thousands of crows flying east, out to their roost by the Saskatchewan Wheat Pool, this endless stream of crows. And then the stream stopped and I stood up, and the blood rushed out of my head a bit, and I looked out at the parking lot and there were no people and no birds—not a breeze—all of this lifeless *stuff*—cars and litter, like the end of the world. I'm not going to the gym any more.

My weight thing? My body obsession? It scares me too, and I don't understand it. I think I thought that if I messed with my body enough my brain would change too, and that would shut off my interior monologue. Maybe I'd become one of those scrawny, sunburnt people in cargo shorts, a nylon windbreaker and hiking boots—those people who go camping for three weeks and eat nothing more than wild cranberries and wild mushrooms—a person who can go out into the wilderness and not freak out about being alone. I used to think Kyle was one of those people, but I don't think that any more.

Him.

I want to stop thinking about this stuff, Roger. I'm so tired. I can't look at Europe on a weather map without feeling carsick. And there was this nutso guy in that grim Parisian hostel, a real religious nut from Belgium, who kept on saying that we each inhabit two worlds—the real world and the end of the world. I can't help but wonder what he meant. It's so lame, yet I can't get that out of my head.

Roger, why is it that people wait until the end of a relationship before they say all the meanest shit to each other?

Why do people stockpile their grudges like ammunition? Why does it always have to end so badly?

Bethany

PS: I quit Staples.

PPS: In summation, I enclose a buttering. Bye, Roger.

A Slice of Small-Town Life

Karen Slice felt snug within her housecoat, its comfortable, forgiving flannel smelling of spilled tea, yesterday's bowl of lilies so perfectly arranged in her grandmother's vase, and the yeasty aroma of her two sleeping children, Melba and Crouton. Outside the sink window, still gritty from a long winter (*I must wash it soon—so many small details to remember in even the smallest, quietest lives!*), Karen witnessed spring's blessed spectacle: gentle dandelions giggling with yellow, cumulus clouds like chunks of raw butter and, sadly, a pair of crows nesting in the linden tree, their black, greedy beaks like the Jaws of Life, except in this case they were the Jaws of Death.

Uh-oh . . . yet another year in which I won't be able to venture outside.

On the counter were two Pyrex bowls in which her soon-to-be-born new children were rising, and they filled the space with a warm, nurturing, floury aroma. Karen Slice felt safe in the kitchen, a room that never made the newspapers, perhaps, but one in which some gentle and important thinking took place. Karen heard Melba's delicate baby snores down the hallway. Soon, Melba would be up and full of beans, as would little Crouton—a crusty devil if ever there was one, so much like his father.

Outside a crow cawed, and Karen shuddered. *Why does death always have to make its presence felt? Can't we take a holiday from death, if only for a day?*

She looked at the rising dough—her babies to be—and was shot with a pang of almost Zen energy, an awareness that death and life were folded together in a complex origami of existence. *But what shape would the origami take? A tree, perhaps . . . or a goose!* Karen had seen documentaries on TV of geese in municipal lagoons greedily inhaling entire bread loaves in genocidal frenzies; swans were even worse. No, the complex origami of life would have to be shaped like . . . an oven. *Without ovens there would be no life.* She went to the bowls to test her unborns for firmness. She felt like . . . like . . . like a wheel within a wheel within a wheel.

Karen realized she needed a buttering. *Getting old is so difficult. The staleness; the lost elasticity of youth. One blinks, and before one knows it, it's onions, sage, perhaps a bit of sausage and a turkey's greasy carcass.*

She caught sight of herself in the microwave's black glass. *Karen Slice, there's still a bit of vim left in you. And don't forget you've got two chil- dren, a husband who cares for you and, shortly, some buns in the oven. Count your blessings.*

She heard the crows cawing outside. They'd seen her through the window and were gathering in the trees and shrubs in an act of menace, but Karen had long ago learned to meet their taunts with indifference.

She was about to brew some tea when she

heard a noise that made her crust freeze—the sound of baby Crouton scampering down the rear hallway, followed by the back screen door's gentle *thwack*ing sound.

He'd gone outside. *Crouton!*

She ran to the door to see Crouton in the backyard, the crows above in a frenzy, swarming in from the east.

"Crouton! Come in!"

"No!"

Karen ran into the yard, screaming, "Crouton, hurry, the crows will eat you! You must go back into the house!"

Crouton ran farther away, into the base of a forsythia shrub in full bloom, a place where the crows wouldn't go.

Karen followed him a moment later, and they stood there together, catching their breath.

"Crouton, what were you thinking? You can't stay out here in the yard."

"But Mother, I can't stay inside the house forever."

"But you have to, Crouton, or else the crows will eat you. You'll die."

"But Mother, staying inside the house forever— that's not really life, is it?"

Karen had no choice but to say the following words: "No. You're right—it isn't."

They both shivered. It was cold out.

"Come inside, Crouton. I'll butter you."

"Yes, Mother."

Roger

Bethany, Bethany, Bethany . . .
You know what I was doing when I found out what you'd done to yourself? I was sitting in a chair in my place. Wayne was in the kitchen, and I was looking out the back window, at a patch of sky in between the front of my landlord's snowmobile and the remains of his above-ground swimming pool. It was almost dark out, but not quite— we're so close to the shortest day of the year—and I was watching that last little bit of blue turn colourless. And then I heard footsteps coming down the driveway towards my door. It was your mother—yes, your mother. Lately she's been bringing me food, and I've been her sounding board for her worries about, well, *you*. Until tonight I've been hiding from the door's knock and we've been swapping notes, but tonight something inside me changed, as if some frozen lake inside me had thawed—I felt *life* returning to me—and so instead of heading into my room to avoid the door, I went to answer it. Yes, it was indeed your mother, and in her left hand she was holding a clear plastic produce bag containing a twelve-pack of Juicy Fruit gum and several airline-sized mini Scotch bottles. In her right hand she was holding a cellphone on which she'd just heard news from the hospital about *you*. I didn't know

this. But there was your mother, and she was in shock and so worried she was making squeaking noises. Wayne, sensing something wrong, bolted towards us, with me trying to keep your mom steady, prying the gum and Scotch from her hands and bringing her into my apartment to calm her down and find out what the heck was going on.

Bethany, Bethany, Bethany. What were you *thinking*!

Okay, Roger . . .

. . . take a breath.

You're asleep. Your mother is back at your place, fetching some things and, I hope, trying to get some sleep herself, but I doubt she will. This hospital room smells like old magazines. I hate this place, and I hate it even more because there's all this depressing Christmas crap all over the place, and you'll love this: You know what I'm thinking about right now? I'm thinking about that joke you made last summer back at the store when we opened a carton and found a thousand Christmas-themed mouse pads—you asked how it was that everything the Italians do using their national red, green and white colours looks Italian, but when we non-Italians use them, all they ever look is Christmassy. A random memory from the Bethany File.

Okay, here's something else from the Bethany File, triggered by some kerfuffle I just heard out in the hallway: Wouldn't it be funny if someone had Tourette's syndrome, but it was a low-grade case? They'd walk around all day saying *Sugar! Sugar! Heck! Heck!* and bystanders wouldn't have a clue what was going on.

Ha ha.

That's not a funny joke, and chances are somebody on the planet has made it before. But I'm not in a funny mood!

How could I be? Bethany! What the hell! I asked your mom why, and she said she didn't know—the poor woman is terrified. And it's not like I know either—geez! *Fuck*! All your mom said was that when the bus driver found you at the back of the bus you were barely coherent but that you said you were sick of being you—that you didn't like who you'd become.

Bethany, *nobody* knows who they are when they're young—nobody! You're not a full person yet! You're liquid! You're lava! You're a larva! You're molten plastic! And don't take that the wrong way. I mean, it's not like it gets much better as you get older, but when you get older—and you will—you'll at least figure out who you are a *little bit*. Not much, but some. And when it happens, you might not be too thrilled with who it is you are, but at least you'll know. But right now? At your age? Again, don't take any of this personally, but no!

Remember back when we started writing I talked about what I was like when I was younger—but then I stopped talking about it? That was because I realized there was no point to it. I did some stupid shit and some good deeds along the way, but it all cancelled itself out and morally I think I'm a pretty generic person, like everyone else. Your Joan of Arcs and Supermans don't come around too often. Mostly, the world is made up of people like me, plodding along. It's what people do—plod, plod, plod. While it kills me to come to grips with the fact that I'm like everyone else, that pain is outweighed by the comfort I get from being a member of the human race.

Let's say you're a judge, or maybe a scientist, and you have your first big case or make your first big discovery, and you become world-famous—you're a genius! But then you get older and stop discovering new things—you've hit your peak. And then you start seeing people enter your courtroom or laboratory or whatever, and they're all repeating the same mistakes as all the people who've ever come before them. And a chill passes through your body. You realize, *Oh, dear God—this is it. This is as good or as smart as we're ever going to get as a species. Our brains aren't going to get larger. Our accumulated pile of human knowledge can only be absorbed so much at a time. As a species, we've reached the upper limits of our intelligence . . .*

. . . and then you plod along.

Here's an amusing anecdote from my youth. I used to like playing with green plastic soldiers, but my mom was anti-war (odd, considering what a battle-axe she was) and wouldn't buy me soldiers. I was too young for a paper route to make my own money, and our house was miles away from a store. My father brought me home a bag of soldiers one night, and I was out of my mind with happiness. I began to play with them, but then my mom came into the room, holding a phone with an extension cord, and she sat down and said, "Okay, you can play with your soldiers, fine. But I'm going to sit here, and every time one of them gets killed or injured, I'm going to telephone their mother. Ready? One, two three, play . . ." Well, you can imagine how much fun *that* was.

The point here is that everyone's family is a disaster. Some are noisier disasters, and some are quietly toxic disasters, but we're all in the same boat. I don't know if I agree with you about your family's behaviour defining or limiting what you can and can't do in your life. I think we're born a certain way and our family can influence us only a tiny bit. So *what* if people in your family die? You'll die too! But in your eighties, in a good nursing home, surrounded by loving family members and staff who don't steal your brooches and dilute your morphine.

Who do I think I am to lay any of this on you? Frankly, the knowledge of who I am is all I have, in every sense of the word. It's the one thing I can speak of without fear. It's the one thing I can give someone else. I earned this knowledge, dammit! And I'm your friend. And your mother loves you too—nay, *adores* you—and she is a terrific woman, and I think she deserves to be allowed to care for you and care *about* you. All the tea in China couldn't make me go through my twenties again, but at the same time I'm jealous that you have such a broad swath of life ahead of you. Needless to say, you'll make many more mistakes along the way, and I fully expect many of them to be highly amusing. I urge you to keep me in your loop, if only to provide me with entertainment at someone else's expense.

Bethany, the world is a beautiful place. Life is short, and yet it's long. Being here is such a gift.

And there's always going to be someone knocking over the Sharpie pen cardboard display in Aisle 3-South. So go over there right now and clean it up!

Your friend,
Roger

DeeDee

Dear Roger,

Now you're the one sleeping. Bethany is having a shower down the hall, and I'm sitting here on this amazingly uncomfortable chair, coping. I'm certainly better now than I was last night. Bethany's groggy and a bit sheepish. I'm not a hundred percent sure she wanted to succeed. She OD'd on a bus, and to me that sounds like she didn't fully mean to. Besides, I think she's so malnourished and over-worked that one painkiller could have wiped her out. As a child, she'd eat the most amazing things (potting soil, daddy long legs, road salt) and always come out fine, so her constitution is rugged. She's got a stomach like a cement mixer.

Roger, I didn't mean to snoop, but I read your letter, and it was lovely. I know *exactly* what you mean about growing older and knowing who you are. How do you explain that to someone so young? By twenty-five you know you're never going to be a rock star, by thirty you know you're never going to be a dentist, and by forty there are maybe three things left that you can still be—and even then, that's only if you run as fast as you possibly can to try to catch the train.

Me, I have two options right now. I can continue life the way I live it now, or I can take Bethany's advice in a note she left me on the kitchen table and remortgage our place and spend the proceeds on school, which is exactly what I plan to do. There was nothing malicious in the way Bethany wrote the note, but she was clear in telling me that my current path is death in disguise. Well, what about her! Between you and me, we are going to padlock her to the admissions office door of the local college and make sure she's on a launch pad to someplace, anyplace, better than right here and now. My eyes are open and can never be closed again.

I can hear her coming back down the hall.

Roger, maybe you want to change who you are too. Do you want to form a club together?

Bethany is so lucky to have met you.

Thank you.
DD

Bethany

Roger,

Okay, trust me, I couldn't be more embarrassed. BUT on the other hand, you'll never guess who came to visit me a few hours ago. Yes, that's correct, Greg. Weeooo!!! Talk about weird. Someone from das Shtoop tipped him off. He walked in the door when I was at a low point (hospital food; yes, I'm eating again), and he was holding a bouquet of daisies with that blue dye in them, and the first thing he said to me was, "Okay, I know, I know, it's those cheesy daisies with the blue dye in them, but I looked at the orange gladiolas they had downstairs—the other option— and they were like something you'd see at your grand-mother's funeral. That is, if your grandmother died in 1948 and the funeral was filmed in CancerVision. Who chooses the flowers in this place—the Mummy? And I could have gotten you an It's a Boy! or an It's a Girl! bouquet, but they were grim. If I popped out of the womb and saw one of those things, I'd say to myself, *Man, this planet's one uninspired place*, and head right off to heaven." Then he looked at me, and I looked at him—and his Ask Me About My Zoloft lapel pin. "So. Bethany. I hear you tried to kill yourself. Interesting. As I mentioned, the world is an uninspired place, but it can have its perks. The first thing we're going to do, young lady, is get you back into some black lipstick, pronto. There's a biker down the hall who got knifed, and her girlfriend is definitely the Black Dahlia sort. I'll be right back."

Once he came back to the room with his loot, I applied it and he said, "Now that's *much* better." Then he went on a rant about people who use the word "passionate." Someone in the elevator had used a phrase to the effect of: *Do only what you feel* passionate *about in life*. I paraphrase Greg here: "I think this is an alarming trend, Bethany, this whole 'passionate' thing. I'm guessing it started about four years ago, and it's driving me nuts. Let's be practical: Earth was not built for six billion people all running around and being *passionate* about things. The world was built for about twenty million people foraging for roots and grubs." (By this time, he was sitting down and eating chocolates that belonged to the woman in the coma in the bed beside mine.) "My hunch is that there was some self-help bestseller a few years back that told people to *follow their passion*. What a sucky expression. I can usually tell when people have recently read that book because they're a bit distracted, and maybe they've done their hair a new way, and they're always trying to discuss the Big Picture of life and failing miserably. And then, when you bump into them again six months later, they appear haggard and bitter, the joy drained from them—and this means that the universe is back to normal and that they've given up searching for a passion they're doomed to never find. Want a chocolate?"

I said, "Greg, I feel like we're on a date or something," and he said, "Yes, Bethany—a date with *death*."

Oh, Roger, I think I'm in love.

B.

Glove Pond: Kyle

"I'm afraid I'm going to have to fire you, Glo," said Leonard Van Cleef.

"You *what*?" asked Gloria.

"Precisely what I said. You're too old for the part, you're too rotund for your costumes, you can't remember your lines and, as of late, your looks are, well, there's no other way to put it, falling apart."

Kyle had never seen Gloria and Steve truly at a loss for words, but there's always a first time.

"Well," added Leonard, "if you two boozehounds have nothing further to say, I'll gulp the rest of my Scotch and leave you." He finished his drink, put down his tumbler and looked at Kyle. "These two basket cases have to be good for at least one novel, kiddo. Strip-mine the hell out of them." He walked to the door. "'Night all."

Kyle looked at Steve and Gloria, and suddenly he felt sadder than he'd felt in years. He didn't want to be in the room but couldn't think of a quick exit strategy. He didn't want to look at Gloria's face but felt compelled to do so—not to look would be ruder. Her eyes were moistening and pink. Her hands were poised on her lap. Her posture was excellent. She was in shock. Steve sat down beside her and reached over and patted her knee.

Kyle realized that Brittany had been gone for a long time—when was she coming back? How much fresh air could the woman need?

Gloria stirred. "I know what I'm going to do," she said. "I'm going to go out and find Brittany, and I'm going to ask her to perform cosmetic surgery on me so I can be young again. I can change things. I can fix myself. I've read brochures. Women's Lib has changed everything. We can do many things now that we never could before. I'll sell the silver to pay for the procedures." She stood up and looked towards the door. "And while Brittany's fixing me up, she can remove whatever it is that's bothering my spleen."

"You'll never find her," said Kyle. "She's a speedy walker."

"Well, I can try." She turned and looked at Steve. "The next time you see me, I'll be young and beautiful again."

"Gloria—"

"No, Steve. I must go." She wove her way through Kendall's plastic toys. She grabbed a coat from a hanger and walked into the night. For a few seconds, the house felt as quiet as a photograph, and then Steve looked at Kyle and said, "What would you do right now?"

Kyle shrugged.

"You're too young to know, anyway," Steve said, surveying the plastic surrounding them. "Are you and your wife ever going to have kids?"

"I'm not sure if we'll stay together."

"Kendall was a good kid."

Kyle had no idea how to deal with Steve's charade. "I'm sure he was."

"You think Gloria and I made him up, don't you?"

"I never said that."

"You wait until the world messes with you for a few more years, Kyle. Wait and see." Steve walked to the door. From the closet, he removed a thick navy peacoat, which he buttoned up. He put on a deerstalker cap and turned to Kyle. "You have a good night. I'm going to look for my Gloria." He left.

Kyle walked around the living room. It had the air of charged blankness that haunts all rooms immediately following a party. Every chair and every nook held a recent memory. He tried to piece together the evening by darting his eyes from door to door, from glass to glass. And then he remembered Steve's study, and he felt a chill. He headed for it, feeling as though he were in a cave, cold and wet and alone. He felt like he was holding a candle and that his sole link to light and humanity was only a puff of breath away from vanishing. There was no sound as Kyle walked down the hallway and into Steve's study, unchanged since his visit an hour ago, and probably unchanged for decades. He walked to Steve's desk and looked at it, contemplating the bottom drawer and its secret.

He sat down in Steve's chair.

He contemplated the drawer's handle.

He thought about writing.

He thought of how people in books are never based entirely on only one person, and of how characters evolve along the way—of how he sometimes created characters in a story and didn't know why, but he had to trust his guts and run with that character. He thought of how, sometimes, a character he thought was based on one person was actually based on another person altogether, and of how far along in a book he could go without understanding that.

Did Kendall ever exist? Were Steve and Gloria gaga?

He realized that Brittany wasn't coming back. He felt like a beautiful glass vase with a chip in it.

He looked at the oak drawer. *What*, he wondered, *could have happened to two people to damage them so badly? What sort of event could warp them, or any of us, to the point where they became mere cartoons of the real and whole people they once were?*

He opened the drawer, but its contents made no sense to him. He felt as though he was looking at Mount Rushmore or Niagara Falls. He felt like a tourist in the world, dropped here like Superman, not belonging, never to belong. Evidence of his fall from grace lay before him now inside a dusty oak drawer—nothing cosmic and nothing poetic that might describe the sadness of life and the unending pain of the human condition, merely a bright orange twenty-five-foot-long extension cord. *What the hell is* that *doing there?*

Glove Pond: Brittany

Brittany Falconcrest continued her walk out into the night, and as she passed by some late-blooming crocuses, now covered in frost, she had an epiphany that in life there are two different kinds of walks. The first is when you walk out the door and know you're coming back. The second is when you walk out the door and know you're never coming back.

The city looked far brighter than it had mere hours before. Sound was crisper, and rather than looking dead, the world looked like it was merely falling asleep and dreaming.

What about Kyle? He would be fine. He would be damaged, but he would be fine, and what's wrong with a bit of damage? The previous Christmas he'd been obsessed with finding the perfect tree, while Brittany had wanted a tree with character. Kyle was now a tree with character. *Big deal. He's a big boy now.*

Brittany was standing on a street corner, contemplating this idea, when a bus stopped beside her and opened its doors. The driver looked down at her. "Come along now, young lady."

The bus interior looked bright and toasty warm. *Well,* thought Brittany, *I may not know where I'm going, but what the heck—I might as well get there faster.* She hopped on the bus, wondered if she should sit at the back or up front, and then decided to sit down just behind the driver.

Glove Pond: Steve

Steve walked towards the light of the main commercial strip—speed-walked, really—past a cluster of teen thugs igniting Roman candles, then around a street corner, where he found a car on fire, a Hyundai, its burning core so bright that the coloured houses surrounding it shone white. The night was still, and the smoke from the car rose in a perfect column, its flames almost silent, sounding like a balloon with a slow leak. Steve followed the plume upwards with his eyes, and behind it he saw klieg lights from a theatre a half-mile away—a premiere! What better place to find Gloria? As he walked to the theatre, dozens of police cars raced past him, their cherries flashing, their sirens muted.

By the time he reached the theatre the premiere was over and the klieg lights had been switched off with a volley of electrical poundings. The street was dark. Steve decided to continue his search into the centre of town. When his eyes readjusted to the night, they were filled with saturated neons from store signage and a continuous stream of car lights, those sturdy white and red beacons. Inside a restaurant, he saw tables covered in white linen and burning votive candles, and a set of triplets sharing a birthday cake that was alive with dozens of blazing white sparklers. He looked to his right, and there was Gloria, standing there too, watching the triplets and their cake and their white light. She was crying, and Steve said, "Gloria, don't cry. There's no need to cry at all." He put his arm around her and said, "Come with me. I want to take you somewhere."

"Where?"

"It's a surprise."

Steve took Gloria around the corner, where a fountain was shimmering with candy-coloured lighting, and said, "Over there, across the plaza—" and Gloria asked, "What's that?" and Steve replied, "Let's find out."

It was a white building, lit from below like a cake in a movie, a cake from which a titanic chorus girl might at any moment explode.

"Come inside," said Steve.

Gloria looked over and saw a plaque indicating that they were entering a planetarium. "Steve," she said, "what is this about?"

"Shush." He took her by the shoulder and, while the staff wasn't looking, they slipped past a burgundy velvet cord and down into a long, dark, muffled hallway. "Through here," he said, and they opened a door and walked into a universe pure and clean, the stars like puddles of baby formula spilled across the heavens. They were the only two people in the planetarium, and Steve asked Gloria to sit down beside him, and so she did. From within the planetarium's central apparatus a cog whirred and a lens twirled and the central projectors sprang to life. Steve took Gloria's hand, felt how cold the rings were on her fingers. Together, they watched a swath of northern lights dash across the universe.

Steve turned to Gloria and said, "What if it turned out that you and I weren't even human—what if it turned out that you and I came from some other planet, far away? What if it turned out that you and I were aliens, different from everyone else on the planet, and that everything we did was thus supernatural and profound—even the smallest of our daily acts would be filled with grace and wonder and hope—wouldn't that be something!"

"It would," said Gloria.

"And what if we threw away everything we have now—our house, our books, our stove, our carpets, our *dust*—and we started again somewhere new, cut ourselves away from the past and headed into the unknown like a space rocket—wouldn't that be something?"

"I'd like that very much, Steve. That *would* be something."

Steve heard only his breathing and Gloria's. The stars kept their silence. Steve nudged Gloria, "Look, it's the Big Dipper."

"It is."

"And over there—Orion."

"Yes, it is."

"You know, Gloria—"

"Hush, Steve."

"Why, my love?"

"Because sometimes words can kill what it is we have right now."

"But, Gloria, I don't think I've ever told you this as such, but I think you're very . . . *beautiful*."

Gloria squeezed Steve's hand, and then Steve remembered something he'd kept in his trouser pocket all day but had forgotten. "Good God, how could I forget something so simple?" He reached into his pocket and removed a small package, and then held an offering up to Gloria. "Gloria, my dear—*gum?*"

Roger, as your instructor, I have to tell you that the truly good author creates a novel so true that it loses the voice of its individual author. We all strive to write "the universal book," one so good that it seems unauthored. Your *Glove Pond* (Roger, what sort of name is *that*?) has a voice that is too idiosyncratic. You need to lose your ego and create a work that speaks in the voice of the "Platonic everyman," not only the voice that you, Roger Thorpe, create.

Your characters also seem like real people, which might sound like a compliment, but don't jump to that conclusion. Characters need to sound as if you made them up, or else people won't feel as if they're reading *writing*: bold, ballsy, *masterful* writing—and they won't feel that they're meeting people who couldn't otherwise exist were it not for books.

Locationwise, your book takes place in your own day-to-day world, and that's *wrong*. Books must be set in an imaginary places—otherwise, how will a reader know you've used your imagination? And I *know* you worked at Staples, Roger, so it's really not fair to the other writers in this class who tried to locate their books in different, exotic, *imaginary* places. Hilary set her fiction assignment in a vampire's cave—now *that's* a location. Dhanni set his collection of free-association verse on another planet; that takes *work*. Staples? I can go there any time and experience it myself. I don't need or want art that tells me about my daily life. I want art that tells me about somebody—*anybody*—else but me.

As a side note, I also think it was inconsiderate of you to mention our class's exercises in bread buttering. Your classmates tried hard to empathize with the buttered bread slice. After you left last week's session, some of us stayed behind and had a discussion about your attitude towards your bread. In the name of making better art, I have to tell you that we found your attitude a bit . . . smug. Who says a piece of bread can't have a soul, a sense of drama or a point of view? Julie's buttering had me almost in tears thinking about its plight. André's buttering made me yearn for a stronger United Nations. Yours just left us . . . cold.

However, I think there is some hope for you—this book you've written can be used as a teaching aid in class. I'd like to distribute chapters of it, and then we will, as a group, analyze them, then go in and remove offending bits and replace them with what we unanimously agree are creative solutions. Only then can your characters crackle with life, and only then will readers feel they've visited a new place, met new people, joined their quest!

I don't think I'd try to publish this, Roger. You'd only be setting yourself up for disappointment. I've written several books, one of which was published, so I think I have some authority on this subject. My book of collected short stories, *Mama's Cranberries* was published by To Catch a Dream Press and won the 2004 Eileen Braithwaite Memorial Trust Prize for Fiction Dealing with Equality.

I am a fan of the arts, Roger—I love art and culture and music—and don't we all? It gives life colour and meaning. We writers—I feel I can speak to you man to man here—inhabit a giving, loving, feedback-filled community rife with generosity and selfless bonhomie. When something good happens to one writer, *all* writers read about it and rejoice! Take *that*, TV! Take *that*, cinema! Take *that*, Internet! We writers will never go away! We are strong!

Now, I feel I have to ask you why you're not contributing to the coffee jar. It may be just a few quarters, but they all add up, and I don't feel it's my responsibility to subsidize my class's "habit." Please, at the next class, remember to pony up your share of the funds.

You did finish a book, Roger. I'll give you that. If you like (and I don't think this is stepping out of any boundaries here), I can supply you with private editing at a rate of $40 per hour, which is the going fee for editors with my credentials. There would also have to be a "rereading fee" for me to once again go through your novel, but that, again, is standard practice.

See you at next Wednesday's class,

Ed Matheson, B.A.

Creative Writing Instructor and winner of the 2004 Eileen Braithwaite Memorial Trust Prize for Fiction Dealing with Equality

www.edmatheson.com

Douglas Coupland was born on a NATO base in Germany in 1961. He is the author of the number-one international bestseller *JPod*, soon to be a TV series, and eight earlier novels, including *Eleanor Rigby*, *Hey Nostradamus!*, *All Families Are Psychotic*, and *Generation X*. His books have been translated into 35 languages and published in most countries around the world. He is also a visual artist and sculptor, furniture designer and screenwriter, as well as the author of *Souvenir of Canada*, its sequel *Souvenir of Canada 2*, and *Terry*, the story of Terry Fox. He lives and works in Vancouver.